THE GLASS BRIDGE

MARGA MINCO

The Glass Bridge

Translated from the Dutch by
Stacey Knecht

PETER OWEN · LONDON

U.S. DISTRIBUTOR
DUFOUR EDITIONS
CHESTER SPRINGS,
PA 19425-0449
(215) 458-5005

ISBN 0 7206 0719 1

Translated from the Dutch *De Glazen Brug*

PETER OWEN PUBLISHERS
73 Kenway Road London SW5 0RE

First published in Great Britain 1988
© Marga Minco 1986
English translation © Peter Owen Ltd 1988

Photoset in Great Britain by Photo·graphics
Printed and bound by WBC Bristol and Maesteg

For
Bert, Bettie and Jessica

One

1

It had been impossible to find out anything more about Maria Roselier. At the time I couldn't ask anyone about her. I had to make do with the impression I had formed of her, based on such scanty information as her date of birth and the place where she had lived. More than twenty years passed before I finally went to Avezeel, a village whose existence had been unknown to me when the name was mentioned. It turned out to be in Zeeuwsch-Vlaanderen, right near the Belgian border.

In the autumn of 1943 I was once again obliged to move to a new address. I had been living in Haarlem for three months and was just beginning to feel somewhat at ease when, one evening, we received word that I was to be picked up the following morning. I dreaded it, especially after the experiences I had had during a previous move.

It rained heavily all night long. Showers pelted against the window and rattled in the gutter. When the weather had been like this in the past I would curl up under my blankets with a sense of well-being and fall asleep instantly. Now it kept me awake for hours; tossing and turning and shivering, I lay and listened to it. The next morning, still shivering, perhaps fearful of what might be in store for me this time, I packed my travelling-bag. But my spirits lifted the moment I saw him standing at the foot of the stairs. There was something in his bearing that immediately inspired trust. In his blue gabardine raincoat and with an old school-bag under his arm he gave the impression of wanting to be as inconspicuous as possible. He told me his first name only, did not ask for mine, and suggested that we walk calmly to the tram-stop. He probably thought I hadn't been outside once in all those months.

During the ride nothing unusual happened; it wasn't crowded, you heard little conversation and, apart from the conductor, nobody walked up and down the aisle paying extra attention to the passengers. The few people who got on along the way had no aim other than to ride in the tram. We had seated ourselves at the back of the second carriage next to the sliding door. I looked at the grey sky, the clusters of bare trees, and the fields, unfolding nearly black with moisture as soon as we had left the city. Twice, on the embankment to our left, a train overtook us and twice, just for a moment, it seemed as if we were standing still. My companion sat opposite me reading a carefully bound book. His straight brown hair fell diagonally across his forehead; now and then he brushed it back with his fingers, but it kept falling forward. As we neared the last stop he closed the book, put it in his bag and nodded at me, smiling. 'We're here.' His upper lip showed the beginnings of a narrow moustache, which he was obviously growing to make himself look older.

After more than half a year I was back in Amsterdam, this time in another neighbourhood, a quiet street in New South where Carlo had found an attic room for me. It was a bare space with a dormer window set into the single sloping wall. Besides a bed the furnishings consisted of a kitchen table and chair, a makeshift draining-board with an oil stove, and a couple of crates full of kitchen utensils and other household goods. Carlo showed up again the next day with a 'Salamander', a small coal heater, which began to roar as soon as he had lit a few newspapers. 'It draws well,' he said. That same week he provided me with a supply of egg-shaped coals and coal briquettes, several ration cards and a bag of food. I did not ask him where he had got it all or how he had come by the money. But it was more difficult for me to avoid making references to the identity card he had promised me. It was to be my third.

In the house below, Carlo told me, lived a woman who ran a beauty parlour in the neighbourhood. She was away all day. Only after I had been there a month did she appear at my door. She just wanted to know – she could barely keep track – who was living in the attic now? By that time, luckily, I was able to introduce myself without any qualms.

During the first weeks Carlo came by frequently. In the beginning he usually stayed no longer than ten minutes, rolled a cigarette, asked how everything was and whether I needed anything, and then disappeared with a wave of his arm. I gathered that he was deeply involved in the Resistance, though he never said a word about it and was otherwise not very communicative. He did tell me that he had terminated his English studies when all students had been required to take the loyalty oath. At times he reminded me of my brother.

Daniel had had to give up his studies much earlier. They were about the same age, had the same build – tall, with broad shoulders – and seemed to be cursed with the same restlessness. Carlo's manifested itself in an abrupt breaking off of conversations and a hasty retreat, while my brother, in an equally unexpected manner, would sit down at the piano or reach for his banjo. That was how they broke free of their surroundings, drastically, unceremoniously. It seemed to me that Carlo loved jazz as much as Daniel. He had a portable gramophone in his room and a large collection of records. I would gladly have listened to them, but that just wasn't possible now.

Sometimes, when he had brought me a bagful of books at my request, he stayed longer to talk, mainly about our reading. A passport picture, my fingerprints and a signature were all he wanted from me.

I hadn't always been so fortunate.

2

He had demanded a considerable sum of money, but the contact man had assured my brother that the papers would be indistinguishable from real ones. Daniel had ordered them for himself and Louise, to whom he had been married for a year. He showed them to us the day they came to say goodbye. As 'Jan and Els Akkermans' they believed they would now be free to go wherever they pleased. They left the city to look for lodgings somewhere on the outskirts of Hilversum.

In the first year of the war we had moved to Amsterdam. I knew that, with one thing and another, my father had suffered losses. That's why I objected when he offered to approach the contact man on my behalf. He would not be dissuaded. He wanted to begin by selling several pieces of my mother's jewellery. She agreed to the plan and gathered the jewellery together. What difference did it make? she sighed. She never wore it any more.

Wouldn't the money be enough to provide all three of us with false identity cards? My father wanted to wait and see how the transaction went with Mr Koerts. I went along with him to the imposing business office on the Amstel River, and as we walked he suggested the possibility that Koerts, a man with many connections, might also know of some safe hiding-places. In any case, my father was planning to ask him about it; after all, he had helped Mr Koerts more than once with various business matters. But we soon realized that Mr Koerts was interested solely in the jewellery. After the sale he raised the subject of the silverware. Should we want to sell that as well, my father was welcome to drop in again. Perhaps then he might know of something for us.

The way home took us longer, but it was not so much the biting east wind that slowed us down; it was as though we were in less of a hurry now that we had lost several of our cherished family possessions. Near our house we stopped and stood by the arched bridge. It was glazed with a completely transparent layer of ice, in which you could see the reflection of the sky. I have often wondered what made us hesitate before walking on to the bridge. Was it merely the slipperiness that held us back?

'Come, we must cross over,' said my father. He took the first step.

'Careful!' I grabbed his arm.

We edged our way slowly towards the middle, where my father placed both his hands on the railing and looked down. On the sheet of ice below us was a seagull, standing so still that it seemed to be frozen on to it. The steel shutters of the brewery on the other side were closed, and their dull-grey, peeling surfaces were a desolate sight. In the bend of the canal the crown of a broken tree hung over the ice.

I let go of my father's arm, pushed off and slid, my arms widespread and my knees slightly bent, down the other side of the bridge, then turned, expecting him to come gliding down after me the way he always had when I was younger. But he didn't follow. With one hand still on the railing he stood gazing past me, as if unaware that I had left his side. I wanted to call out to him, but I stopped myself. Standing there motionless in his dark-grey jacket and grey hat, my father seemed farther away from me than just those few feet, as if he had put a much greater distance between us and no longer saw me. I tried to dispel that image by latching on to another I had of him, one that belonged to my earliest perceptions. Holding his hand, I had learned to walk; sitting on his knee, I had looked at the drawings in his sketch-book, illustrations for the stories of an enchanted world which he, his left arm securely around my waist, conjured up for me. Most of my youthful memories revolve, not around my mother but around him.

I loved my father. Every day, for years, I picked him up at the railway station. Even before he had made his way from the platform to the exit he would wave to me with his hat, which he usually held in his hand. He always arrived at the same time. On the one occasion when he had had to take a later train, I had waited, sitting on the back of my bicycle and looking with a certain resentment at the passengers who had arrived earlier.

Our route home never varied. We would walk along the shabby houses in Spoorstraat, across Heideveldstraat, and past the house of the Roozen family, a shrunken, elderly couple with two unattractive daughters. The eldest daughter would quite often be standing in the doorway as we walked by, so that my father would have to stop and inquire about the health of her mother, a sickly woman who limped. The daughter was in her late thirties, had a pointed, yellowish face and an upper lip covered with dark hair. From atop the high stoop she kept continual watch over the railway crossing visible at the end of the street, so as not to miss any of the passing trains. I always prayed that her mother wouldn't come shuffling towards the front door, her cane thumping against the wooden floor. As a young child I had been afraid of her, and something of that fear still lingered. Even before my father had ended the conversation I would be walking on, but he would quickly catch up with me and lay his hand on mine.

Now I saw his hand clasping the bridge railing. I saw his blue-grey eyes tearful in the wind, and behind him the broken tree with its network of black branches.

3

Ruth had come along early one morning. She didn't have much time, just wanted to speak to me in private, and whispered, as soon as I had closed the front door, that she knew of something for me. Everyone was sitting downstairs in the living-room drinking coffee, a daily ritual ever since my aunt and uncle had had a houseful of people staying with them. We remained standing in the dimly lit hallway. I knew her from the art school, where she had been one of the most gifted students. At first I thought she had come to ask me about a new drawing club. The idea appealed to me, because now that the primary school, too, had been forced to close, I had a lot of time on my hands. I had got the job through my uncle, who knew the headmaster. They had had a shortage of teachers but had wanted to keep the school open for as long as possible.

'Just keep them busy,' said the headmaster, a man with black, horn-rimmed spectacles and bristly grey hair. 'A set curriculum is obviously out of the question now.' He gave me a class of about twenty children who, on the first day, regarded me curiously and somewhat disbelievingly. In an attempt to look older I had put my hair up in a bun, but I doubted whether that helped. They sat in the front row, sometimes three to a bench, so that the classroom seemed even emptier than it actually was. Walking to school that morning I had been trying to decide what we should draw first: a house, a ship, a kite, something they could copy easily. Once there, I suddenly thought of the drawings my father had made for me and my hand moved of its own accord across the blackboard. A boy with curly red hair asked, 'Is it going to be something funny, Miss?' They looked at me gravely, as if I had come to tackle a difficult problem. I began drawing a broadly smiling clown in a striped suit, using all the coloured chalk in the dish. 'A circus!' I heard them shouting behind me. And that's what it became. I urged them to think up other things that belonged in a circus. The following day they started drawing as soon as they entered the classroom. Their enthusiasm grew, even though they number of children in the class was dwindling every day and one child would sometimes have to finish a drawing that had been started by two or three.

Ruth had come for a different reason. In a conspiratorial tone she began talking about a place in the country. Would I be interested in going there? 'For goodness' sake, say something, Stella!' she exclaimed, poking me in my side. 'What do you think?' She bounced up and down with impatience. Her long bangs fell in her eyes, which she kept focused on me, half squinting. I had often seen her sitting like that in class before she began to work on a drawing.

I nodded and asked myself why she had come to see me just now. Since the closing of the school I had seen her only once, by accident. From behind the living-room door I could hear the deep voice of my uncle. He was undoubtedly reading something aloud again from the *Jewish Weekly*, the umpteenth series of regulations, warnings and prohibitions. I had moved in with him after my parents were picked up and deported.

When we had last met I had told Ruth about it. I had stayed after school longer than usual that day. I straightened up the classroom, put the children's drawings in a folder, cut paper and distributed it in the hope that all the children would still be there the following morning. I wiped the blackboard clean, got fresh chalk out of the supply cupboard. Then I watered the plants, even the ones in the classroom next to mine where the teacher had not shown up that morning. On his table lay an open botany book and a sheet of paper covered with notes. He had already prepared his lesson.

In the building hung a silence I wanted to break. I walked through the corridors, up the stairs, looking into the other classrooms. On the blackboard in the sixth-grade class was a complicated multiplication exercise. I slid into the front bench and took a pencil and pad out of the desk. For more than half an hour I remained in the school. I don't know why; I did not have the slightest premonition, not the slightest idea. On the way to the front door I picked up a forgotten jacket that was lying on the floor and hung it on the coat-rack, tucking in the left side with the star on the pocket. I stood still for a moment in the doorway, as if I didn't know which way to go. I decided to call at my uncle's house before going home, to bring him a book the headmaster had asked me to give him, which had been sitting in my bag for more than a week. As I left the building I remembered how, in my own student days, I had always raced out of the door if I had had to stay late. Now I felt no need to hurry. With my collar turned up against the freezing wind I took a detour along the park, which I never walked past any more because, after all, we weren't allowed in. The bare branches of the bushes poked through the railing. I broke off pieces here and there and then threw them back. The ducks huddling together at the edge of the pond flapped their wings agitatedly. It seemed as if they wanted to fly upwards but were being restrained by something. The wind chased the withered leaves across the paths, through the half-frozen puddles where seagulls marched about briskly. It blew fiercely against my back, making me quicken my steps.

A man who lived opposite us came to tell my aunt and uncle: at four-thirty they had cleared out several houses, my parents' house among them. At that very moment I had probably been sitting in the school building working on the multiplication exercise, and looking to see whether the answer was divisible by thirteen. It hadn't been.

Ruth now displayed her impatience in another

manner: she rubbed her arms and pinched them. 'I think it would be perfect for you,' she said, 'or have you already got another address?'

'No, not yet.'

'It's really safe, believe me.'

'Of course, if you say so.' I was overcome by the same feeling of uncertainty that had assailed me at the school door. 'May I think it over for a day or two?'

Clearly surprised by my reaction, Ruth again began trying to talk me into it. I would have to decide that same day, she didn't have all that many addresses.

'When would I have to go?'

'Tomorrow morning. You'll be picked up.'

'Has that been arranged already?'

'It certainly has. Either you go, or somebody else will.'

'Where is it?'

'In West Friesland. On a farm.'

'Oh.' I didn't like farms, the smell of manure, walking around in wooden shoes. But I couldn't say so to Ruth. 'It's pretty short notice. I'd have to make the necessary arrangements.' My evasions were too artless. I wanted her to know that I was grateful for all the trouble she had gone to; she was taking great risks for me. 'I'll do it, happily, that goes without saying, and I'm glad you thought of me. But I'd like to discuss it with my aunt first. There are all kinds of practical things . . .'

'Let me know this afternoon what you decide. I'll be home till four. Then I'll be leaving, too, and you won't be able to reach me any more.' At the door she turned and asked, again in a whisper, 'Do you know Roelofs?'

'No. Who's that?'

'If anything comes up – I mean, you never know – you can always phone him.'

She told me the telephone number, repeated it twice and said, almost inaudibly, 'Don't write it down, memorize it.'

That was no problem for me. I am good at memorizing numbers, and seven and thirteen hold a special significance for me. The sum of Roelofs's telephone number was divisible by seven. I watched her leave. Outside, her red-brown hair gleamed like copper. The broad pavement was bathed in sunlight. It was the end of April, a mild spring day. Children ran outdoors with skipping-ropes, balls and scooters. At first they moved about rather timidly but soon they were engrossed in their games. The adults went strolling from one corner to the other and back again. They were willing to risk it. The Saturday morning tranquillity and the inviting weather apparently misled them into thinking that nothing could go wrong.

4

They were still sitting around the table, and I had the impression that they had been joined by several newcomers. Perhaps it seemed that way to me only because, in the past weeks, I had stayed away from these gatherings. I had grown tired of the discussions, which always revolved around the same issues: the war, soon to be over now that the Germans had been beaten back in Russia, the new measures, the instructions from the Jewish Council, the relatives and friends who had been taken away. They rarely laughed and, when they did, it was because of some comment made by Mr de Beer, in his grating voice. This time he was talking about an advertisement for labels, bearing one's first and last names, to sew on to clothes and blankets. 'Labels,' said Mr de Beer, 'labels! What'll they think of next? Aren't we already marked?'

Everyone laughed except his wife, who was in the habit of taking her husband's jokes seriously. 'It's just so you don't lose anything,' she said concernedly.

'Many people are as yet unaware of the fact that it is absolutely essential, in case they should be required to leave unexpectedly, to have all their baggage packed and ready,' my uncle read aloud, his glasses half-way down his nose. The *Jewish Weekly* lay spread out in front of him.

'Of *course* you have to have something ready,' said Fred Boston. 'You read that in the paper all the time. Backpacks are preferable to suitcases. Clothing must be sturdy and practical.' He sounded as if he were dictating, and he added emphasis to his words by rapping his fingers against the edge of the table. The three Boston brothers occupied the front room on the second floor. Fred was the youngest. Because of his work with the Jewish Council, he considered himself something of an authority on the subject.

I had gone to sit on the piano-stool and watched my aunt as she went around with the large coffee-pot. Each time she bent over to fill a cup she let her hand rest briefly on someone's shoulder. Her long silver necklace swung back and forth. The locket clicked against the pot.

Because I was still thinking about my talk with Ruth, about the urgency with which she had advised me to leave, I barely heard anything else that was said. I did notice that the voices were more subdued than usual. There were longer silences, as if they were withholding more from one another, keeping their misgivings to themselves, not daring to penetrate to the heart of the matter. And then that sudden burst of laughter. Mr de Beer simply couldn't resist continually drawing upon his inexhaustible repertoire. My uncle removed his spectacles and rubbed his grinning face. My aunt put down the pot and gave Mr de Beer a jovial nudge in the back. Someone slapped the palm of his hand on the table, making the cups rattle.

'So, Fred, what do the fellows at your office have to say about it?' asked my uncle when they had finished laughing.

I didn't wait for Fred's answer. 'I have to go upstairs,' I said to my aunt. 'See you later.'

That afternoon I found her alone in her room. I had been trying to finish the drawing I had been working on for a few days, but without success. I had ripped it up and begun packing my travelling-bag with the same things I had packed into it months earlier when I had been given the false identity card and there was talk of the three of us going into hiding. There was to be just one more meeting with an intermediary, but he had never appeared. A week later it was all over. The owner of the cigar shop diagonally opposite us had seen the razzia truck driving up to our door. 'You must make sure that no one ever forgets this!' my father had shouted to him before he stepped in. 'They searched the place, too,' said the shopkeeper. 'Probably thought you were still in there hiding.' A couple of days later his son had managed to get my bag out of the house.

My aunt sat by the window, crocheting. 'Your uncle's gone over to see an old friend. It's very possible he can help us. He's got contacts.'

I had heard it all before. It was as though we were all walking around in a cramped circle, as though everything you said within that circle was then repeated by somebody else, as though, within our limited freedom, we had an equally limited vocabulary at our disposal.

She laid her crocheting in her lap and looked outside. 'The trees seem to have turned green overnight.' She said this in the tone of voice of someone who realizes that her hair has turned grey overnight. In the sunlight the creases around her mouth were sharper and I now saw, too, the network of lines under her eyes.   'Were you just going out?'

'Yes, in a minute.'

'Sit down for a while. I'll make us some tea. Or are you in a hurry?'

'No, not really.' I kept my coat on when I sat down opposite her, as if that would make it easier for me to tell her that I would be leaving the next morning. I couldn't tell her yet. I felt ashamed.

She crocheted another row. Was she still making doilies? The entire family had been amply supplied. Whenever I stayed at her house I saw how she pinned them to large pieces of cardboard. They looked exactly like spiders' webs.

'Remember when we used to go to Heck's Lunchroom?'

'On Saturday afternoons, do you mean?' She pushed aside the lace curtain. 'I thought I saw him coming. No, I suppose not.'

'We weren't allowed to tell my father about it.' The three of us would walk across the Rembrandtsplein. When we crossed the street my mother and my aunt would each give me an arm. 'Shall we?' my mother always said when we stood in front of the revolving door, which was operated by a doorman in uniform.

'Your father was quite conservative.'

'Oh, he wasn't so bad. He was very tolerant.'

I was still trying to work out what had been going through his mind as he stood in the middle of the ice-covered bridge looking past me. Had he been about to turn round and go back to Mr Koerts, to give it another try?

'Your mother certainly didn't mind, though. She adored pastries, she could eat three at a time. I don't know how many times I must have told her, "You're getting too fat!"'

My mother and her sister were only two years apart, but my aunt, slender as she was, with her golden brown curls and bright-red lipstick, looked much younger. She held her crocheting in front of her, motionless, and I knew she was thinking about other times, just as I was, about events that seemed to be buried deep in the past even though they had occurred no more than four or five years earlier. Everything which had happened before the war belonged to that past. Her gaze had strayed back to the window.

'He's been gone a long time, don't you think? He was supposed to return at three-thirty.'

'Is it as late as that already?'

We turned simultaneously towards the clock on the mantelpiece. It was twenty minutes to four.

'You haven't had any tea.'

'Never mind.' I stood up. 'Maybe I'll run into him outside.'

'Be careful, Stella.'

I still hadn't discussed my plans with my aunt. I

resolved to tell her as soon as I had been to see Ruth. She lived nearby, ten minutes away at the most. If I left now I should be there just in time.

'There he is!' My aunt jumped up and at the same time clapped her hands to her mouth. The crocheting fell on the floor. 'My God, they're cordoning off the street!'

5

Only when I was on the roof did I realize that I should have warned them, or at least called out to them, to give them a chance to prepare themselves. Everyone had probably been home at that time of day. But I hadn't seen anyone as I walked up the stairs; I had heard only the sound of voices coming from the Bostons' room.

When the latest ordinances had been discussed downstairs, Fred and Herman – Jaap, the eldest, rarely showed his face – had looked around them with an air of *This doesn't concern us, that's for other people*. And when someone warned that you had to take care not to be transported once you were in Westerbork,[1] Fred gave such detailed advice that it seemed as if he were speaking from personal experience inside the camp. But even then, one could hear the conviction in his words, This doesn't apply to *us*, of course.

In response to my question to Herman about

[1] Westerbork: Dutch labour camp (as opposed to an extermination camp), located in Drenthe.

whether they might go into hiding, I received a simple answer: they were *gesperrt*, exempt. Fred had seen to that. Herman, I thought, could walk out of the door with no problem at all, without even wearing a star. Nobody would take him for a Jew. With the round, bald spot on his scalp, the fringe of pale-blond hair, his white face and watery eyes, he looked very much like a monk who never went out into the open. 'All you have to do is put on a habit and you can walk right past them!' He had to laugh at that. No, he preferred to stay at home keeping house for his brothers, as he had ever since their parents had died, years before. One of his most cherished pastimes was ironing – trousers especially – for whoever wished it. He even did my skirts.

'Girl, you look awful! Here, give me that, might as well since I'm standing here anyway,' he would call out from behind the ironing-board. With his fleshy hand, the one with the blue-black thumbnail, he would lift the iron, spit on the underside, place it squarely on the damp cloth and rapturously inhale the rising cloud of steam. He usually sang songs from German operettas as he worked. 'Wenn die kleine Veilchen blühen' and 'Irgendwo in der Welt gibt's ein kleines bisschen Glück' were his favourites. The moment he heard my footsteps in the corridor he would call me in to show me the knife-edged creases in the trousers of our housemates.

'Now they can really step out in style,' he would say. Humming, he would hang the garments carefully on clothes hangers, pat them playfully and nod with satisfaction. His brothers dressed well. He himself walked around in an old pair of trousers and a threadbare housecoat that smelled strongly of boiled cabbage.

Fred was ten years younger than Herman. He had a bicycle licence and cycled every morning to the Jewish Council office.

'What do you do there all day?' I asked him once.

'I do work that needs to be done,' he replied sternly. He hoped I realized how truly important a job he did. Compiling lists of the Jews who were still around, for example. He had his hands full with that chore. Today, a hundred and eighty more names could be crossed off. Haven't we forgotten to add the Hellman family from Majubastraat to the list, Mr Boston? Would you have a look at that please? And Fred had had a look. Yes, indeed. The boss was right, he had forgotten the Hellman family. A couple with four children: Louis, aged twelve; Rozet, nine; Ester, six; and the baby Gonda, eight months. That really gave him a headache! The whole alphabetically arranged list had to be retyped. Sloppy work was unacceptable.

Jaap Boston was a serious, reticent man whom you only ever saw in the living-room, reading, in his favourite chair. It was difficult to make any contact with him. On the few occasions he went out it was to buy books in a particular antiquarian bookshop. If he met you in the corridor he would touch his dark fedora, smiling apologetically, and then hurry up the stairs holding a parcel under his arm. He owned all the works of the German expatriates, the Manns, the Zweigs, Roth, Wassermann, Neumann, forbidden books which he had covered in brown paper, just to be on the safe side. I was allowed to borrow them.

At first I felt drawn to Fred, the youngest of the Bostons. He was my age, we lived in the same house and the evenings were long. Sometimes he came over to bring me a book from Jaap. I soon got bored with these visits, though, because the moment he came in he would proceed to tell me stories about the pretty blonde girl-friends he had had to leave behind in Zwolle, the town where the Bostons were born. He confessed that he never so much as opened a book and, glancing down at my drawing and painting materials, said that he had better things to do with his time. Was I listening? The war would be over any day now and, when it was, he would head straight for America, where fortunes were waiting to be made. His little speeches never lasted too long. He made them while walking back and forth in my small room. After a quarter of an hour he would consult his watch and say that he had to run; if Herman asked for him, he was just going for a short walk. He would wink at me and sneak downstairs.

The occupier had imposed a way of living on us to which Fred could not adjust, and I suspect that the only reason he worked for the Council was because of the *Ausweis* they gave him, the pass that entitled him to go out in the evenings. Whenever he came home too late, as he usually did, storming up the stairs, slamming the doors and screaming at his brothers, who reproached him for his reckless behaviour, his housemates would shake their heads. That Boston boy would come to no good.

He suffered the same fate as everyone else in the house. *Gesperrd* or not *gesperrd*, it no longer made any difference: a Jew was a Jew. Clad in freshly ironed trousers they stepped into the razzia truck. No doubt Herman watched them with satisfaction. *That* was how you were supposed to dress when you went travelling. The sharp creases stayed sharp for some time – at least, as long as there was enough room to sit comfortably.

6

It had become quiet, both inside and out, but there was something artificial about the silence. I stood in the doorway of my room, my bag in my hand, waiting for the sounds that would inevitably follow. They failed to come.

I put my bag down, tiptoed to the staircase and listened again. It was as if I were waiting for a sign, a signal, and I remembered how, in the past, standing on a deserted platform, I could be relieved from a feeling of uncertainty by the whistle of an approaching train. Suddenly everything happened at once: the doorbell was pressed and held, the outside door was bashed open, the dividing door was smashed against the corridor wall, the stairwell shook with the thundering of boots.

I took my wallet out of my bag and hid it in my coat pocket, crept up the stairs to the attic, pushed open the trapdoor and lowered it softly behind me. Climbing out of the attic window, I hoisted myself up on to the gutter and then crawled upwards along the roof tiles to the wide chimney. I stretched out behind the chimney, my head hidden in my arms, as though by not seeing anything I should not be seen. Now commands rang in the street, followed by the shuffling sound of people walking around and around in a circle. You could tell they were afraid of having to go in a certain direction. Orders put an end to the continual circling. The slamming of car doors resounded against the eaves. The house beneath me shuddered once more from top to bottom, as if all the air were being forcefully pumped out of it. At that moment I began slipping, but just managed to grab on to an iron peg that was sticking out of the chimney. Carefully, to prevent the tiles from coming loose and falling in the gutter, I pulled myself up and flung my arms around the cement structure.

The entire operation could not have taken more than fifteen minutes. They were in a hurry down below. Perhaps they were standing there with stop-watches in their hands, trying to break a record. Years later, before I had set off in search of Maria Roselier's background, I had the sensation of having landed in a similar situation. I was in a foreign seaside resort, sunbathing in an outdoor café. Suddenly clouds gathered overhead, the sky turned black as ink, a whirlwind sucked water and sand upwards into spirals, and within several seconds everything around me had been blown away. Groups of tourists fled, pushing and stumbling over one another, into waiting buses. Their cries subsided when a man shouted a few brief orders. I had thrown my arms in front of my face. When I lowered them, everyone had disappeared. I was left standing on the deserted promenade amidst a chaos of dismembered pavilions, devastated awnings and severed palm trees.

After I had heard them ride away, another silence fell in the street. Even the birds were still; they remained in hiding. How long I lay there, I don't know; it may have been half an hour, an hour. I had completely lost all sense of time. Eventually I sat up with my back against the chimney, looking around me at the hilly landscape of blue-grey roofs. The copper cupola of the Diamond Exchange gleamed in the afternoon sun. I saw the windows on the upper floors of the Jewish Nursing Home, whose drawn curtains suggested security within, and the little white tower on the corner house, which seemed to be keeping a look-out for me. Small clouds floated by, effortlessly changing form as if to set me an example. Two pigeons alighted on the gutter and began to coo. Were they trying to let me know that the coast was clear?

7

The conversation lasted no more than two minutes. I barely had to say a word, I could come immediately. He had spoken in a measured voice.

He had told me to come to his apartment, near Vondel Park. On the landing I met a man in a white shirt, with salt-and-pepper hair, an unhealthy complexion and piercing eyes behind rimless spectacles.

After I had cleaned myself up at the wash-basin in the hallway – I was given bandages for my bruised palms – and brushed the dirt from the roof off my jacket and the dress that Herman had ironed for me, the man led me to an office, where he directed me to a chair facing his desk. The top of the desk was covered with paperwork and files. We sat by a window that did not look out on to the park, as I had expected, but on to a courtyard with a blank wall. He looked at me for a while without saying anything, then bit his narrow, unnaturally red lower lip.

'You sure as hell fooled them,' he said finally, with a short burst of laughter. His cheerfulness, which seemed so inconsistent with his obvious aggravation over the telephone, annoyed me. The bandages tugged at my palms.

Someone had silently entered the room. 'This is Anna,' Roelofs told me.

It was only when she came and stood next to me and handed me a cup of coffee that I saw her, a girl with short, dark hair and slightly bulging eyes. She stared at me as I drank my coffee, then turned brusquely and walked with graceful, soundless steps out of the door. Her wide, brightly coloured skirt swung at her hips.

The few times I recollected her I wondered whether there had been distrust, or even animosity, in her gaze. At that moment I had been unaware of it. In those circumstances one paid no attention to such details. Perhaps I was mistaken. I never had the chance to speak to her and it wasn't until the summer of 1947 that I saw her again, in the Leidseplein. She was sitting in the outdoor café of the Hotel Americain, engaged in lively conversation with a slight young man wearing spectacles. A child with reddish curls sat beside her. I don't know whether she recognized me. In any case, I didn't bother going over to her. Was I afraid of the confrontation? Of memories that might be stirred in both our minds? In later years I repeatedly caught myself avoiding people whom I had met during the war, people who had done their best to help me and perhaps expected something from me in return. Who knows whether they did? I never looked them up.

Roelofs sat chuckling and tapping his pencil on

the blotter. It made me nervous. He asked for my identity card, which he examined closely.

'We'll have to replace this. It's lousy. If they caught you with this card, you'd be in trouble.' He stood up and put on a dark-blue jacket. 'We can go right away. You're lucky, I've got a good address for you. The bus leaves in fifteen minutes.'

'Where are we going?'

'Not too far outside the city. There's room on a farm.'

'A farm?' So it was going to happen after all. Had it been only that morning that Ruth had come to me with the same offer, which I had been so reluctant to accept? It seemed like weeks ago.

'Yes, why? Would you prefer a hotel room? I know *I* would – with you in it!' He laughed loudly now, his shoulders shaking.

That evening, when we had turned into a fairly dark, tree-lined country road several yards from the bus-stop, he planted himself directly in front of me and pulled me towards him. I was totally unprepared – on the way, in the bus, he had said little, mostly gazing out of the window – and however hard I struggled, he had me in his grip, dragging me to the roadside and into the bushes, where he tried to pin me to the ground. Among leaves and prickly branches I felt his breath on my face, heard a wheezing that sounded like someone with bronchitis. He succeeded in pulling my coat open, but when he shoved his hand under my dress I beat and kicked him off me, hitting him wherever I could.

'You're a wild one – God, you're really a wild one!' he panted. 'Let's sit down, come on.' But I had already wrestled myself away from him and started running. I heard him coming after me. His heavy footsteps reminded me of the clip-clopping of a horse. 'Stop!' he shouted.

I had come to a fork in the road, and he took advantage of my hesitation to catch up with me. This is all wrong, I thought fleetingly, he's one of them, I've had it. He grabbed my arm. I immediately pulled it back and kept my distance.

'Just tell me where it is. I'll go there myself.'

'No, no, I'll take you,' he said. 'They're expecting me to. Come on, let's go.'

We walked the rest of the way in silence.

On the farm that night, lying in my box bed, where I had finally fallen asleep after hours of tossing and turning, I dreamed of my father. I saw him in his dark overcoat, hat in hand, his greying hair wind-blown, a half-smile on his lips. He was walking towards a high, rounded bridge that I thought I recognized, but it stood in a setting completely unknown to me, a desert-like landscape in which there just happened to be a bridge. It spanned no water and joined no banks. As my father drew closer to the bridge, he began walking more slowly, and then stood still, moving on his heels and toes as if he were marking time. The bridge was slender and airy, almost transparent; the piers sank away into a cottony vapour, like cows in a low-lying mist. I stood on the other side beckoning to him, but he didn't see me and made no attempt to cross the bridge.

8

He persisted, and I couldn't avoid him. Within a week he had furnished me with ration cards and a new identity card. 'I've also been able to get your stuff out of the house,' he said. 'We stop at nothing!' The fact that he had my travelling-bag was a surprise to me, but I didn't let it show. In the months that followed he visited me regularly, acting as if nothing had ever happened, as if I valued his presence. Each time I saw him walking towards the farmhouse I felt frightened, and each time I made sure he didn't catch me alone.

One afternoon, when I was out behind the bean field cutting spinach, he was suddenly standing beside me. It was hot, approaching the end of July. Working on the farm suited me more than I had thought it would. In the beginning they had let me do the lighter chores: weeding the vegetable garden, feeding the chickens, sweeping the barn. Later I was put to work on the land, and learned to walk in wooden shoes, handle cows, tolerate the smell of manure. Evenings were more difficult, when the doors of my box bed were shut behind me. In the cramped pitch-darkness I felt like some object locked away in a cupboard. It gave me nightmares.

'So, I've finally got you alone,' said Roelofs.

'Come to help with the spinach?'

'Actually, I had something more pleasurable in mind for this afternoon.'

'Bad luck, Roelofs, I've got to finish this bed!' I shoved the basket forward and continued cutting.

'I was thinking of a different bed. In the hay.'

He was walking so close behind me that I stood up straight.

'Why exactly are you doing this work?' I asked.

'I like Jewish girls.'

'I've noticed.'

'I enjoy taking risks for them.'

'I've noticed that, too.'

'Where are the farmers?'

'On the land. Shall I call them for you?'

He laughed, a short burst of laughter which, as I had noticed when we had first met, was accompanied by a spasmodic movement of his shoulders.

'Go ahead, they won't hear you anyway.' He tried to put his arms around me.

I walked to the stable, grabbed a pitchfork that was lying on top of a wheelbarrow and turned round. He was still standing in the same place among the beanpoles, his back towards me, the long leaves like a wreath around his neck. Then I saw what he was looking at. A German army truck was approaching along the country road; it slowed down and stopped at the path leading up to the farmyard. Roelofs tried to appear relaxed, his hands in his pockets, his head tilted slightly, but I could see that his body had gone rigid. In the truck sat four helmeted soldiers who all turned their heads towards us at exactly the same time. The dog ran out of the shed and barked, a couple of chickens scratched and pecked indignantly in the yard, but apart from that, nothing stirred between us and the army truck. The sun blazed and there was not a breath of wind.

One of the soldiers got out of the truck and came walking up the path, without his helmet, the collar of his tunic open. He walked stiffly but unhurriedly. The path was about thirty yards long. I saw that Roelofs had picked up the basket of spinach and was walking, stooped, across the field. As the soldier walked, he made small holes in the sand, which immediately filled up again. His boots were covered with grey dust and his heels clicked together when he stood in front of me. He asked if I could possibly give them something to drink – water or milk, it didn't matter which. It would be extremely *liebenswürdig*[1] of me, seeing as how it was so *furchtbar heiss*.[2] He unhooked a canteen from his belt, whereupon I nodded and acted as if I had only just understood him.

After the glare of the sun, it was difficult at first to distinguish one thing from another in the dimly lit kitchen. I had to search for the milk jug, which had been placed in a bucket of water. Gropingly, I poured it into the dented canteen, felt the liquid

---

[1] *liebenswürdig* = charming.
[2] *furchtbar heiss* = frightfully hot.

running over my hands, heard it splattering against the tiled floor. Half of it ended up there. I filled it to the top and dried it off.

In the truck I saw them passing the canteen around, drinking in turn. It took quite a while, and the entire time I kept myself busy sweeping the ground, so furiously that the chickens flew about in all directions and the dog scampered back to the shed. As they drove away, the soldiers made a gesture that caused me to put down my broom. They all saluted at exactly the same time.

When they had disappeared round the bend, Roelofs stepped out from behind the beanpoles. His face was ashen.

'Would you like a drink, too?' I asked.

'Have you any coffee?'

'We always have coffee here. They keep it warm in a pot on the oil stove.' I called the mixture 'farmer's blend'. It tasted strongly of chicory, but it wasn't bad if you added warm milk. I filled two cups and sat down opposite him at the table.

'He probably mistook you for the farmer, don't you think?'

'You can't stay here.' He drummed his fingers on the blue-checked oil-cloth.

'If he'd noticed anything suspicious about me, they would have been back by now.' I looked out of the window, there was nothing to see. It was safe for me to remove my kerchief.

'I don't trust them. They'll be back.'

'But my papers are in order, aren't they?'

'You can never tell what they'll do next. They

might begin patrolling the polders. It's too risky. I'll have to find another address for you.'

'And I was just getting used to it here.'

'You'll be picked up tomorrow. I'll arrange it. Make sure you're ready early. I myself can't come.'

'Thank goodness for that.' It slipped out. That was not the kind of thing I should have said to him; it had the opposite effect.

'You know you want it. I can tell. You're a clever little bitch.' He stood up slowly, wiping his forehead with his handkerchief. The colour had returned to his face; he was even beginning to turn red. The coal stove was still burning – they had cooked on it two hours before – and dense, hot air poured through the hole in the kitchen door. But I barely noticed it. The heat was nothing compared with the stifling nights in the box bed.

'You were pretty scared just now, weren't you?' I wasn't afraid of him any more, I knew I could handle him. I simply had to take care not to let my dislike show too clearly.

'If I was scared, it was for you. You're a damned good-looking girl. But you know what it is with you? You ask for it by keeping me at a so-called distance!' He had walked round to my side of the table and tried to grab me.

'Don't you dare!' I seized a chair and held it upside-down in front of me. For a long time it had been bothering me that I had not decided, that evening on the country road, to forbid him helping me in any way, to continue on alone, not accepting any papers from him, nothing. But often it's only afterwards that you know how you should have acted in certain situations.

'All right, all right, calm down,' he said. 'Look, I've gone already, see?' He walked backwards towards the door.

The next morning, bright and early, I was picked up by Lies – at least, that's how she introduced herself. Roelofs had said that he would send a woman, 'because it's you'. She thought it better not to take any luggage, just the essentials. Once again I left my travelling-bag behind.

The weather had changed. Clouds hung dark and low as we walked the mile to the bus-stop. Everything was wet with dew, and the coolness wafting in on a gentle breeze was a relief to me after my last night in the cupboard. Lies talked on about plantain, ragwort, coltsfoot, sow thistle and other plants she observed growing alongside the ditch, as if she were taking me on a nature walk. Fortunately she never stopped to get a closer look. Resolute, hands deep in the pockets of her raincoat, she walked beside me. She wore sandals with short woollen socks. I had on the same shoes, now battered and worn, in which I had crawled across the rooftops.

Lies brought me to Haarlem and dropped me off just outside the centre of town, in a side-street, at the house of a couple who welcomed me like a long-lost daughter. A week later she came to tell me that, several hours after my departure, the

Grüne Polizei[3] had raided the farm and ransacked the place. The farmer's wife had been sensible enough to distribute the contents of my bag immediately among her things.

I had disappeared without a trace.

[3] Grüne Polizei: uniformed German police.

9

It had not sounded very convincing, I thought, but she didn't seem to have noticed. I had been standing in the doorway with my coat on when she came upstairs.

'Maria Roselier,' I said.

'Lina Retty,' she said. Her hand was supple and cool. 'I thought it was time we met.' She wore a checked suit, was heavily made up and had doused herself liberally with Soir de Paris. 'You always wonder who's living above you, and people do seem to come and go up there in that attic. Are you planning to stay awhile?'

'Oh yes. I like it here.' What I liked even more was the fact that she had waited until now to visit me, but I obviously couldn't say that to her.

'What do you do?'

'I study, and I draw a bit.'

'Well, I shan't be in your way much. During the day I'm at the beauty parlour, and this house is practically sound-proof. Do you ever hear anything?'

'Never.'

'My clients will have to wait out in the street this

morning, I'm afraid. I have to go to the dentist for a filling. What a nuisance!' She pulled her face into a little grimace, then quickly replaced it with the professional smile with which she had greeted me at the door. 'Were you just leaving?'

'Yes.'

I had rarely been out since I had come to live there. Carlo had advised me to remain inside until I received my new identity card. The day before, he had dropped in to give it to me. And now I had been ready to go for nearly an hour, but I couldn't overcome my hesitancy. Several times I had opened and closed the door, walked to the window, looked out, seen a couple of children with a skipping-rope and a man pushing a wheelbarrow, nothing more – and returned to the door. With the document in my hand I had, for the umpteenth time, repeated to myself the various facts that accompanied my new identity. Even when I had learned them backwards and forwards, I still wavered. Miss Retty's arrival clinched the matter. We walked together down the stairs.

From the moment I had seen it, the name on the identity card had intrigued me. I had asked Carlo whether he had made it up himself.

'No,' he said, 'it's an existing name.'

'Did Maria Roselier just hand over her identity card to you?' This procedure was new to me. On my previous papers all the information had been fictitious, there were no personal backgrounds involved and I had never thought twice about any of it. But this time somebody had lent me her name and I found that disturbing. I wanted to know how he had arranged it.

'It was fairly simple.' He said down beside me at the table. 'Let's get this over with first.' He opened a small box with an ink-pad inside and took my hand.

'She was born in 1919. We're two years apart.'

'She's no longer alive.'

I was stunned. It was as though he had informed me of the death of someone I had known well. 'Was she so young when she died? How did it happen?'

'I don't know. I wasn't able to find out. We removed her card from the Register Office file and replaced it with a new one. That means she's not dead, not officially.' He hadn't let go of my hand.

'Did she have an accident?'

'I told you, I was unable to ask.'

With the same practised movement he had demonstrated when I had had to put my fingerprint on my passport photographs, he pressed my right forefinger on to the ink-pad and held it above the identity card.

'Careful now, make sure it lands in the middle of the box. What slim fingers you have!'

'Perhaps she did, too. Were you able to see on the card when she died?'

'Yes. The date struck me – 11th May 1946.'

'A Saturday. On 4th April she had turned twenty-one.' I had been nineteen then, and the war two days old. My father and I had walked to the end of our street, because there were rumours that French troops could arrive at any time. The entire neighbourhood had gathered on the street corners to await their coming. The first motor cyclists stopped right in front of us. They carried heavy packs, wore greenish brown jackets and bronze-coloured helmets. Their sweaty, oil-smeared faces looked tense. They had apparently lost their unit and asked where the fighting was. 'Not here yet,' said my father. 'The front is farther east.' He gave them directions for leaving the city. *'Bonne chance!'* I had called after them.

Before I signed the identity card, I practised for a while on a piece of scrap paper until I had found a signature which didn't resemble mine in any way, and which I felt best suited Maria's name: round, solid letters, curving upwards with a certain flamboyance.

'I hope you realize that you now have airtight papers. Here, this goes along with them.'

Carlo placed a form with an official seal in front of me, an extract from the Register Office file confirming my birth in Avezeel. When I in return handed him my other identity card, he reacted just as disapprovingly as Roelofs had at first. He ripped it up, put the pieces in an ashtray and lit them with a match.

'I don't understand. They could have done much better. Very sloppy work.'

'It isn't as bad as the first one.'

'And you paid a lot of money for it too, I bet.'

I had shown it to my uncle. 'Anything's better than the one you had,' he had said. And Ruth had even considered it a stroke of luck for me. 'This is cheap compared with some of the prices I've heard of.'

'Very little was organized in those days. It was only later that it really got going, wasn't it?'

'Unfortunately, yes.'

We stared at the flames, at the shrivelling grey paper. My passport photograph, which had come unstuck in the heat, remained intact the longest. The edges curled, then gradually melted towards the centre. I saw my hair disappear, my neck, my chin and, last of all, my eyes, as if wanting to witness it all for as long as possible. They they, too, were gone. I was not there any more. My sensations at that moment most resembled what you experience after a severe dizzy spell: your head is empty, you think you have come round, yet some part of you is still missing.

'So,' I heard Carlo saying, 'from now on you're Maria Roselier and nobody else. Remember that.'

'I'll try.' I wanted to make her past my own, to act just as she had. But what did I know about her?

' "Try" isn't good enough. You've got to *do* it, you've got to *be* her.'

The authoritative tone he had assumed had a comical effect. I didn't think he was very good at it, and I told him so.

'You're right, it's not really my style. I just wanted to drill it into your head.'

'Where exactly is Avezeel?'

'In Zeeusch-Vlaanderen, near the Belgian border. You're half-Flemish now.'

'Does that mean I'll have to learn an accent?'

'No. You haven't lived there for years. You moved

to Amsterdam. Look at the addresses we've written on your card . . . do you know them by heart?'

'Yes.' I named them. I had lived in two places.

'When the war is over, go down to Avezeel sometime.'

He jumped up and walked to the door.

'I've got to go.'

'Will you come to Avezeel with me? Are you from that area?'

'I can't tell you that. Yes, I'll come with you.' He placed his hand on my shoulder. 'Bye, Maria.'

He opened the door, tugged at my hair and ran down the stairs. Leaning over the banister, I watched him leave. He didn't turn back to look at me the way he usually did.

10
_____

Lina Retty asked where I was heading; she had to catch the tram in Noorder-Amstellaan. I said I had to do some shopping in the neighbourhood and accompanied her to the tram-stop.

'Whenever you feel like having your hair done, come along in. I'll give you a nice little discount. Speaking of hair, you shouldn't keep shoving yours under your hat, it'll dull the shine.'

'I catch cold easily. That's why I do it.'

'You spend too much time indoors, and it shows. You shouldn't stay cooped up like that. A person needs fresh air and recreation, certainly these days. You have boy-friends, don't you? That young man who drops in every so often . . .'

'Oh yes, of course I have boy-friends.'

'And your parents? Where do they live?'

'My parents live in Belgium.' I began filling in the blank pages.

'Then you probably haven't seen them for quite some time.'

'It's been three years. I came to Amsterdam to study. But at the moment most students are working at home – that is, if they're not working in Germany.'

'Yes, poor things. The men are the dupes. We girls are the lucky ones. So tell me, does that mean you come from Belgium?'

'No, we come from Zeeland. From Zeeusch-Vlaanderen. My parents moved to Belgium in 1940.'

'I was just going to say, I wouldn't have guessed it from the way you talk. Actually, you haven't got a Zeeland accent either.' She eyed me carefully.

'Honestly? I'm glad about that. I've been doing my best to get rid of it. Other students often hold it against you if you have an accent.'

'Zeeusch-Vlaanderen . . . I know the place well.'

'Oh?'

'I was in Cadzand once, on holiday. You see lots of those dark-haired types there, like you. Spanish blood, they say. Heavens, there's my tram!'

She ran towards the tram-stop, teetering on her high heels, and just managed to jump on to the rear platform. She waved with one hand and fixed her hair with the other.

I had passed my first test. I was so relieved, I took my time over the shopping and even after that walked around for a while. Back in my room I went over what I had told Retty. I had to remember it word for word, make facts out of my fabrications.

Since my escape, eight months had gone by, and in that time one experience had haunted me as no other: lying motionless on the roof, my arms around the chimney, my face buried. The memory of that immobility must have had a grip on me that morning when I had remained standing at the door. It was a long time before I had dared to lift my head. I didn't notice until later that my hands had been injured; it was my eyes that hurt most, from the sun. The rest of my body was stiff, numb, as if it were weightless.

At my birth I had weighed three and a half pounds. Whenever my mother told me what the scales had shown – and she told me often – she sounded as if she were talking about something she had bought at the grocer's. Thanks to Sister Romslag, the visiting nurse who had taken me under her wing, I didn't have to be placed in an incubator. But I had had to endure the results of her efforts for years afterwards. If we met her in the street, we would stop and I would have to give her my hand. She wore a blue-black dress with a stiff white collar and a blue-black veil attached to a white cap. A silver loignette added extra severity to her bony face. Reluctantly, I would hold out my hand; I was afraid she would take me with her. Let me have little Stella, if you please. Her hand was hard and brick-coloured. It was horrid having to touch it. My mother had no idea how frightened I was. Each time she would push me out in front of her with a mixture of awe and pride, crying, 'Here she is! Now, what do you think?' And then the nurse would nod her approval. With great pains and patience, she had managed to keep me alive, and every time we met I felt I had to thank her for it. Thank you for my being here, Sister Romslag.

But, twenty-two years later, my chances of survival were once again dubious. And yet I had taken risks in Haarlem which I had previously avoided. Why? The transition from the farm to the home of the childless couple Baak had been difficult for me. They liked nothing better than to have me spend the entire day sitting at their living-room table, while they indulged me with tea, coffee and home-made cake. I felt I was suffocating. They obtained drawing materials for me, but I couldn't get a single line down on paper. They brought me books from the library, but I didn't have the patience to open them. I wanted to get out into the street, to break free of their concern, their cherishing, their need for a 'daughter'. I could only feign affection, promise to be very careful, and come home at the time we had agreed on.

After three months the neighbourhood in which they lived was no longer safe; the area was patrolled, houses were searched, and suddenly the streets were teeming with armed WA[1] men. The Baaks contacted Lies, who felt it would be better if I left.

In the days I had wandered through Haarlem – always wearing my hat, my talisman – my indifference had grown. I had made no effort to dodge the Grüne Polizei, who had the entire centre of town under their surveillance. I had visited the streets where the occupiers had their offices and stood in front of the Ortskommandantur[2] building, watching the grey cars come and go. The frequency with which members of the Wehrmacht,[3] Grüne Polizei

[1] WA = Weerafdeling: paramilitary arm of the Dutch facist NSB organization.
[2] Ortskommandantur: local Wehrmacht command post.
[3] Wehrmacht: German armed forces, 1935–45.

and SS[4] walked in and out of the building had been so great, it was as if they had about-faced as soon as they entered the lobby.

I often sat at the reading table in Café Brinkmann, in the Grote Markt, poring over the bombastic army reports, listening to the hum of voices, and I felt included; even occasionally, as if I belonged.

On Saturday afternoon, as I was leaving the café, I found myself in the middle of an NSB[5] meeting. I mingled with the other bystanders on the pavement and heard somebody barking from the platform that had been erected next to the meat market. Why did I do these things? The possibility that I might not be arrested, provided I was careful enough, had not yet occurred to me. Actually, I never thought about it one way or the other. I think I was just curious to see how far I could go.

[4] SS = Schutzstaffe: security guard.
[5] NSB = Nationaal-Socialistische Beweging der Nederlanden: Dutch fascist organization.

11

One evening in the middle of January someone rang my doorbell just before curfew and, even though it was short-long-short, I panicked. There were three possibilities: either the Germans had been tipped off, or Roelofs had found out where I was, or my brother had somehow been able to trace me. I myself had already abandoned all hope of seeing him in the near future. Did he know that our parents had been deported? Was he in trouble too? A visit from Carlo at that hour was improbable. After he had brought me the identity card he had been back only once, and I was beginning to worry that, as far as I was concerned, he had completed his mission.

He came racing up the stairs as if the police were hot on his heels and, panting, stammered out that something had gone wrong. One of the members of his group had been caught. Carlo suspected he had been betrayed. The man was not likely to talk, 'but you realize that they'll do everything they can to get the information they want out of him'. His voice broke when he added that he would have to change addresses immediately, and that he had got away just in time. 'I wasn't followed, I'm absolutely sure about that. I don't live very far from you.'

'I didn't know that.'

'I have to keep that kind of information to myself. Talking can be destructive, and those who know too much are vulnerable. If I could stay here for just one night – after that I'll go into hiding for a while, and then we'll see.'

He had plonked himself into the wicker chair, my newest acquisition, and was rolling a cigarette. His head drooped. 'I was able to take along a few things, but no sleeping-bag.'

'Don't worry, we'll think of something.'

I looked at his thick hair and had to control an urge to run my fingers through it, not as a gesture of comfort, but to see how it felt.

'I can sleep on the floor.' He had stood up and was walking back and forth as if looking for a suitable spot.

'I have two blankets, we have two coats, and I even found a plush table-cloth here in the attic. That'll make a great blanket.'

'You don't mind?'

'Mind? Not at all! I think it's funny, your coming to me. I'm the one who's supposed to be in hiding!'

'You're "Maria Roselier", you mean?'

'Right. I'd forgotten for a moment. And I've been doing so well!' In the past weeks I had completely immersed myself in my new identity. He ought to have been there when I had let my imagination run wild, making up stories for Lina Retty, or when I had practised other ways of walking. Despite Miss

Retty's 'dark-haired types from Cadzand', I pictured Maria as having been an ash-blonde, a tall girl with a spring in her step and elegant movements, traits I felt went best with her name. I identified myself with her in every way I could, even hung the bathroom mirror higher above the sink so I should have to stretch to look into it. In the conversations I had with myself I used a Flemish accent.

'Did the doorbell startle you?'

'At this time of night, yes.'

'We'd agreed on short-long-short, hadn't we?'

'Yes, but it's different when it actually happens.' All that ringing of doorbells buzzed shrilly in my head. The sound had become a sign: the time has come. If I survived the war, I decided, I would never again have a bell on my door.

'I'm sorry about that. It really is a mad situation.' He managed a weak laugh.

'I'm glad I can finally do something for you! Come on, take your coat off.'

Carlo had unpacked an assortment of food he had brought along and was arranging it on the table in a tempting still life. I busied myself preparing supper, relieved to have something to keep myself occupied. I had wished so many times that he would stay longer, and now that he was here I didn't quite know how to act. He was no less shy than I was, I noticed. He masked it by concentrating on lighting the coal heater.

'Hey, where did you get that wicker chair and all those cushions?'

'Lina Retty gave them to me.'

'Oh, so she's been up to see you?'

'She comes here regularly. We've become pretty close. A couple of days ago she knocked at my door without any warning. I was scared to death! Usually she calls out to me if she's on her way upstairs. Apparently she had a leak in her ceiling and wanted to see whether it was coming from up here. When she saw the books on the table, she said she felt sorry for me because I have "so much cramming to do". A little later she brought me the cushions and some tea, and the wicker chair from the attic. When everything's back to normal we're going to spend a weekend with my parents in Maldegem.'

'What are you talking about?!'

'My parents have lived in Maldegem for years. That's one of the stories I've told her. I have to say something, don't I? She's always telling me about her failed marriage, her family crises, and Salon Retty in Maasstraat. If I want to I can get my hair water-waved there. She'll give me a "nice little discount"!' She had also given me an extra key for the front door. 'Easier for your friend,' she had said, winking. Long afterwards my room had smelled of her Soir de Paris.

We ate our supper seated on cushions in front of the Salamander. Carlo rolled cigarettes and began talking about how little we really knew about each other. 'I have to keep so much to myself. I probably overdo it, I admit. But you don't give anything away either, except to Miss Retty. She knows more about you than I do, even if you do make it all up!'

'You call me Maria, too, don't you?'

'That was the agreement. You had to get used to the name.'

'Then it's only logical that I start inventing a past to go along with that name.'

'You don't have to invent anything for me, Maria ....' He smiled and stood up. 'I'd love to know what you were like as a little girl, what you did.'

As he added fresh coals to the heater, the warmth of the fire swept over me, and in the glow I saw our shadows moving, merging, on the sloping wall. It was the first time he had ever spoken to me with such familiarity. His voice brought me back to another January day, long past, when I had gone skating on the canal near our house. Because my skates had come undone, I had wobbled my way to the little stand where hot chocolate was being sold, and held tightly to a trestle. I looked at the gritty, yellowish holes around the piers of the bridge, at the snow-covered waterside, at the elegant homes with their glittering windows which, seen from the ice, looked even more magnificent. Rows of skaters in colourful sweaters, holding each other loosely around the waist, glided past. Someone detached himself from one of the groups, came over to me, knelt down and tightened the straps of my skates. 'Here we go again,' said my father and, our arms crossed, hands clasped, we skated towards the bridge. Despite the low arch we glided under it, ducking our heads, and I caught a glimpse of a mysterious ceiling, a basketwork of joists and beams from which long icicles dangled. Blinded by the light of the afternoon sun we shot out of the darkness, slackened our speed, and were caught up by the others and borne along in their midst.

That was how I began. Carlo had put his arms around me, giving me the same feeling of security I had had on that winter's day in my youth. Days would follow when we could be entirely ourselves.

12

When I began writing the letters, the winter had already passed. For weeks the ice had covered the window-panes like a layer of frosted glass. To keep myself from being totally cut off from the street I had rubbed peepholes on the panes, which immediately froze over again. I had comforted myself with what I had so often heard my father say about that time of year: there is always at least one day in February when you feel that spring is coming.

At first, I was bursting with energy; I walked miles to get coal and petrol, stood for hours in the line for provisions and furnished my room with the various things I had found in Retty's attic. On the base of a standard lamp I placed a shade made of oiled paper. I drew the view, the impervious façade with its uniform windows, the budding trees. I saw them turning greener every day. They reminded me of that last Saturday afternoon when my aunt had looked, shocked, at the newly green elms in front of the house, as if she deeply resented the trees for keeping to the season. I reread *War and Peace*, the two blue-grey volumes that my brother had given me just before he had gone away, and the books Carlo had left behind.

After he had stayed a full week, he had decided to establish contact again with the members of his group. He had to, they probably needed him. He hoped that their strength hadn't been depleted any further.

'Couldn't I be of help?'

'Far too risky.'

'I can distribute ration cards, deliver messages. You work with female couriers, don't you? I want to be useful. I'm just sitting here doing nothing.'

'At least you're sitting comfortably. You don't have to have anything to do with anybody, your rent has been paid for a year in advance, and you have me to arrange the rest.'

'I don't want special treatment.'

'Take advantage of it. It's the only way for now.'

We stood by the door, holding each other close. He stroked my hair, my back, ran his cheek along my forehead. There was nothing more I wanted to say, and yet there was so much I wanted to add to what we had told one another in my narrow bed, the plans we had made, what we would do when the war was over. Even then, he hadn't divulged anything about his Resistance activities and had kept his true name to himself. He thought it better that way. Our names didn't matter.

'How long will you be away?'

'Rather longer this time, I'm afraid.'

He pressed his nose against mine and I saw a

single, elongated, clear-blue eye with two dark flecks in the middle.

'Will you be careful?'

'Yes. And will you take care of yourself, too? Promise me you won't do such idiotic things as you did in Haarlem.' I had told him about my walks past the German offices.

'Word of honour.'

'And I promise to come back as quickly as possible. Goodbye, my darling Maria.'

He released me, picked up his old school-bag and walked down the stairs. When he was almost at the bottom I ran down after him and, in the hallway, we fell once more into each other's arms.

Since Lina Retty's departure the house had become a hollow, deathly still space where I was occasionally startled by an inexplicable creaking and rustling. Lina had come along to tell me that she had closed her beauty parlour. 'I've used up all my best stock and I've got no money to buy more on the black market. Can you imagine me shampooing with that ersatz soap? My clients would be out of the door in two shakes of a lamb's tail.' She was going to move in with her sister in Overijssel. 'You and your friend haven't split up, I hope?' she asked. 'I never see him any more.'

'He's gone to live with his parents in Dordrecht. It's quieter there, he can work better. He'll probably be away for a long time.'

'Why don't you get out of the city too? Where I'm

going, they still have plenty to eat. Haven't you any family at all you can go to?'

'Only in Zeeusch-Vlaanderen. But it's such a trial getting there, I'd rather stay here.'

'To each his own. Anyhow, you'll have the place all to yourself. Take good care of the house, will you please?'

I had promised to take care of it, although I didn't really understand what she expected of me. She had had the rest of the house hermetically sealed.

After six weeks of waiting I couldn't stand it any more. I decided to call Roelofs from the local post office. A woman answered and asked me to hold on for a moment. I couldn't tell whether or not it was Anna, because when we had met she hadn't said a word.

'Yes?' Roelofs's measured voice.

'Do you know anything about Carlo?'

'Hey, is that you?'

'Do you know anything?'

'Yes.'

'How is he?'

'He's sick.'

'Sick?'

'They're keeping him under observation.'

His cryptic tone distressed me, but I asked no further questions; I knew what had happened to Carlo.

Roelofs immediately began insisting that we meet. 'I'd really like to see you again sometime. Can't we make a date?'

Fortunately, he didn't seem to know where I lived.

When I heard him chuckling, I slammed down the receiver.

I had hung the mirror back in its old place so that I should no longer have to stand on my toes to see my reflection. I was sick of the whole game. Why should I continue trying to act like someone I had never even known? I was only fooling myself. And who was I doing it for, now that Carlo and Lina Retty were gone? Carlo had seemed to enjoy the role I was playing. He had drilled it into me, and perhaps not for security reasons alone. Mystifying and camouflaging were part of his daily routine. Sometimes I had the feeling that this was now all he knew anything about. The only sign of life I had had from him was a letter addressed to Miss M. Roselier. Folded around the ration card and money within was a piece of paper with the typed message, *On assignment. To be continued.* Proof that Carlo himself had been able to send it.

As I was tucking the note into the back pages of my writing pad, I discovered a letter I had never sent. It dated from the time when I had lived in Haarlem with the Baaks.

Dearest Hubert,

You're probably amazed to be hearing from me after so long. We had to leave Breda rather suddenly in November '40, and it was impossible to reach you at the time. When I phoned, your mother said you were in Delft. I wanted to ask her whether you'd registered for the Technical

University, but she hung up immediately. Are you going to study architecture after all?

I've thought more than once about that year after we'd done our finals, when we saw so much of each other. Remember the day we went to Rotterdam, sat in the Atlanta Café, saw *Mr Smith Goes to Washington* at the Lumiére in the afternoon, and danced all evening in the Pschorr Nightclub, where Nat Gonella was playing? That lady crooner was singing with the orchestra – Stella Moira, a skinny girl with long hair and dark, slightly crossed eyes. She was wearing a white silk blouse, a short black skirt and a huge red patent-leather belt. We wondered how she could sing so loudly, all laced up like that. She sang 'Georgia on My Mind' while we danced on a floor made of glass tiles with coloured lights burning underneath. You thought I looked like her. We might have the same first name, and maybe even the same hair, but I'm definitely no wisp and I couldn't hold a note to save my life! I did wear those shiny wide belts long afterwards, though. Now I've lost them all.

Not much chance of our coming back to B. for the time being – so much has happened since then. You'll understand, I hope, that I must keep my address a secret.

Bye, Hubert
love, S

I tore up the letter, threw the pieces into the coal heater and lit them with a match. Then I pushed the table next to the open window and began writing other letters. Those, too, eventually ended up in the Salamander.

Dear Anna,

We've met only once, very briefly, and we've never even spoken to one another. I often think about the way you looked at me that afternoon in Vondelstraat. Were you already suspicious when you heard that Roelofs would be accompanying me? You knew him better than I! What happened afterwards still disturbs me. I want you to know this because I feel that we're both in the same dependent position, and it's a situation we've landed in against our will.

Of the three times I've escaped arrest, that Saturday afternoon was the first time I made a decision for myself. Without saying anything to anybody I walked up the stairs and hid on the roof. Just how I ultimately ended up with you and Roelofs, I can barely reconstruct. By way of three rooftops, a fire ladder and a balcony – it's incredible that nobody saw me – I finally reached an open door and walked inside. I stood in a bedroom, hurried through a corridor and down four flights of stairs, then slipped unseen out of another unfamiliar door. Only once in your life, I believe, can you act so instinctively. It's as if you are doing it with your eyes closed.

Yes, I beat him off me. It wasn't hard. I used to box a lot with my brother, who is four years older than I am. He taught me the left jab, the right hook, and the upper-cut. My mother was always afraid he'd give me a black eye, or worse, whenever she saw us standing in the garden facing each other with our fists raised. For years she considered me 'the weak child', the one who needed to be protected. But my brother never really hit me. He'd even deliberately fall backwards into the grass when he thought I'd aimed my blows well. So I was able to defend myself, thank God. What still bothers me is that I stood there hesitating at that crossroads in the polder – and then chose the easy way out. I'd already run away from him. I could have kept on running.

I had to tell you this, Anna. Who knows, perhaps we'll meet again sometime.

Good luck,
S

My dear Dorien,

Sorry that I didn't call or write to you on your birthday. It's the same as last year: I just didn't have the chance. But I did think of you on that day. I'll never forget the date. How could I? It's two days before my mother's birthday!

Remember Mr Walstein? His face popped into my mind when I was thinking about how we used to cycle down Loverlaan, where once we almost ran over him near my house. We found Walstein pedantic, if only because he was a teacher at the gymnasium. To us simple HBS-ers,[1] everyone who sat on the gymnasium side of the school yard was pedantic. He always walked straight as a rod, his nose in the air, and he never said hello to anyone, not even to my parents, though he lived only a few houses away from us. A week after the surrender he suddenly appeared at our door. He had sent his wife and two children to England. When my father asked him why he hadn't gone with them, he said he couldn't possibly abandon the school. He seemed very confused. Several months later he was in such bad shape that he had to stop teaching altogether. Until then, I don't think any of us had realized that he was a Jew. He probably hadn't either. For a while he came by regularly. My mother had long conversations with him in the parlour. She tried everything to cheer him up and bring him to his senses. It didn't help. Shortly before we left Breda he hanged himself in his attic. My mother, who had always thought him an insufferable smart-aleck, blamed herself for a long time afterwards that she hadn't done more for him.

How was your birthday, Dorien? Do you still remember how, one year, your father came to get me when you were staying at the country house? They'd hidden me in a laundry basket and carried me inside. You turned completely red when you

---

[1] HBS = Hogere Burger School: comparable to secondary school. Gymnasium students followed a similar curriculum, with the additional subjects of Latin and Greek.

opened the basket. It was your best present, you said. That was thirteen years ago. These days it would also be a handy way to come and wish you a happy birthday, though I think that now it might frighten you.

See you, dear Dorien,

love, S

Dear Hubert

Looking back, it was better for everyone that we lost touch with one another. I see many things more clearly now than I did then. At first it was rather unpleasant for me to have to accept the fact that your parents didn't welcome our friendship with open arms. But gradually I realized just how opposed they were to your having a Jewish girl-friend. You couldn't do much to change their views, I know that, but nevertheless you were unconsciously influenced by them, and the few times I went home with you it surprised me that you made no attempt to break through that atmosphere of strained politeness. After May '40 your mother, particularly, became downright hostile towards me. A bit more support on your part would have been nice. In any case, I'd have caused you even greater difficulties now. My leaving was a solution for us both.

Bye,

S

Dear Hennie,

The last evening when you visited us in

Loverlaan I should have returned your book, Couperus's *Travels through Ancient Times*. After we moved I discovered that it had accidentally found its way into one of our crates of books! The sudden transition took a lot of getting used to. My father thought living in Amsterdam would be more favourable for his business. Till the very end, he tried to carry on leading 'a normal life'.

My aunt and uncle had found us a house in their neighbourhood. And since Daniel (who in the meantime, as you know, had got married) had also settled in Amsterdam, my parents were thrilled with the prospect of having their whole family around them. Who could have guessed that this would be fatal for them all? At that time there were still few dark clouds on the horizon.

If I ever return, you'll get a new copy of Couperus. And you *must* read the two volumes of *War and Peace* which I drag around with me everywhere I go. Then you'll see which passages I've marked. This one, for example: 'I can't tell you what's wrong. I don't know. No one is to blame,' said Natasha. 'It's my fault. Oh, why doesn't he come?'

All the best, Hennie,
love, S

Dearest Ruth,
Isn't it strange .... That very same evening I ended up on a farm after all. Everything would have turned out differently if I'd accepted your offer on the spot, because then you wouldn't have

given me that telephone number. The idea that, time and again, our decisions are made for us, is often unbearable to me. There are days when I wonder whether what I'm experiencing is actually happening, whether I might not be wandering around in someone else's skin. And once in a while I even dare allow myself the thought that everything will work out in the end. Otherwise, what possible point could there be to our existence?

If we pull through, I hope we'll see each other again one day. I still have that sketch of yours – the Achtergracht, seen from your window. You were by far the best at the art school. Are you still at the address you said you'd be going to that day? Can you get any work done there?

Take care of yourself, Ruth
love, S

Dear Herman,

Of all the people in the house, you are the only one I dare write to, the only one I'd like to talk to now. Not to your brothers, not even to my aunt and uncle – *especially* not to them. I never stop thinking about any of them, Herman, but I can't contact them. I'm afraid to mention any of their names. I shall cast a spell with my silence, keep those names to myself, so that one day they may return to me unharmed.

You were so uncomplicated, Herman, a real softie, always ready to help or lend a sympathetic ear. You were almost motherly. I've always had the impression that what was happening never really got through to you. Or were you just pretending not to know? Was that how you kept it at bay? The way you used to sing 'Schön ist die Welt' – it was as if you truly believed it.

I can imagine how you all must have searched for me in the razzia truck, how you asked one another, 'Where is she? Isn't she at home?' I knew exactly what I was doing, Herman. My actions in those few minutes were completely premeditated. Like a thief ready for anything I escaped.

You may remember how very worried I then was about my brother and his wife. I didn't know how to get in touch with them. And now I'm still unsure. I know they left Amsterdam, yet I still wander through the city hoping that one day I'll bump into Daniel or someone who knows him. Even, if need be, Mrs Benders, Louise's mother. You met her once when she came to the house. She refused to sit down, was very snooty with my aunt and uncle. Later you called her a 'stuck-up old prune'! She tried to get us to tell her where Daniel and Louise were staying. She had a right to know, of course. But she was all suspicion, as if she thought that I was deliberately keeping their address from her.

In the attic room where I now live (I can climb right out on to the roof if necessary – I checked as soon as I moved in) I sometimes imagine that I hear you downstairs singing, that I hear the others rattling around in the house. But there's no one there. It's only the sounds from neighbouring houses that penetrate my walls.

Whatever happens, Herman, you will be with me, all of you, for ever.

A warm hug
from S

Two

1

His tone of voice when he told her 'I've got nothing to say about that' made it clear that he considered the subject closed. Stella had put down her travelling-bag and was leaning with her arm on the bar. Could he not have known her, never have heard of her, in such a small place? She found his surly reaction odd, especially since he had greeted her so heartily just moments before. He turned away and went back to tapping beer, but his piercing brown eyes darted continually in her direction. His skin was red, verging on purple, under a thatch of dark hair. She took him to be in his late forties.

The men sitting around the middle table, who had ceased their boisterous game of cards during her conversation with the innkeeper, now resumed their game in silence.

'How long were you thinking of staying?'

'One day, maybe two.'

'Let me know when you make up your mind.' He gave her a key whose size seemed more suited to the door of a shed than to that of a hotel room. 'Up the stairs, first door on your right.' He walked over to the card-players with a tray of beers.

She waited until he had returned. 'I'd like a whisky please, with a little water.'

'Coming up.'

She carried the glass to a small corner table. The inn, with its pompously framed seascapes hung on dark wallpaper, its plush table-cloths and lamps with parchment shades, had the feel of a living-room. The card-players began talking loudly again after their first few gulps of beer. One of them, a man in a plaid jacket and a lurid green tie, stood up with his glass in his hand and went over to her. He took a pack of cigarettes out of his pocket and offered her one. She said she didn't smoke. After he ('May I?') had seated himself opposite her, he asked where she was from. Up north, he expected. 'Amsterdam – am I right?' She nodded. He was right. It was the same everywhere you went. They all asked identical questions, wanted to know where you lived, what your husband did, how many children you had and, most of all, what your 'origins' were, because, 'looking at you, one would think – I hope you don't mind my saying so – you are not entirely of Dutch descent'. Without wanting to, you supplied the information, as if there were a good grade to be earned. For years she had been on her guard as soon as anyone asked her about her background. The war, the period of chaos after the Liberation, the twelve years with Reinier, from whom she had been divorced for quite some time now – she had never said a word about any of it. Inventing stories about her past had become almost second nature to her;

she had always made sure she had several different versions to fall back on. But lately the stories hadn't flowed as readily. You couldn't continually conceal what you were; you only ended up losing yourself.

The man in the plaid jacket remained sitting there, curious about what she was doing out here in the middle of nowhere. Hoping he would leave once he had received a reply, she told him she was travelling through the country on business. 'I go from one village to the next.' That had been the way she had wanted it. Always on the move; visiting people, talking with them, but no longer than necessary; leaving them behind, no ties; taking her leave of faces, figures, constantly shifting like the fragments in a kaleidoscope, melting into one another and vanishing, over and over again. No single region held any secrets for her any more – except one.

'So you're familiar with this place?'

'No, I've never been here before.'

'For your work. . . . Can I guess?' He took a few swigs of his beer, his Adam's apple leaping vehemently out of his too-tight collar. 'You're a sales rep. In lingerie!'

'What in the world makes you say that?'

'I . . . er . . . I mean, you'd think . . . . Well, what *do* you do anyway?'

'I visit bookshops with a publisher's list.' She had not wanted to be dependent on Reinier. The office job she had been offered hadn't appealed to her at all; she preferred working outside the office. It enabled her to keep up her drawing, too, in her spare time.

'Aaaah, you make visits. That's a coincidence! We've got something in common.' He chuckled.

'Have we?'

'I'm a drug salesman. I visit doctors. Always on the road, just like you.' Jumping up from his chair he made an almost imperceptible movement, as if he were about to take a bow, then changed his mind and sat down again. 'Would you like another whisky?'

'No, thank you. I was just on my way upstairs.'

'Wait a minute – do you mind if I tell you something? There's no bookshop here. They've got a doctor here in Avezeel, but no bookshop!' He slapped his hand down on the plush table-cloth and watched her in amusement, without a look of surprise – the only other expression he seemed to possess – ever leaving his face. He had caught her lying, and the trump card was his. He hadn't managed to play a trump like that at the other table. The card-players pointed to his empty chair and asked him whether he had forgotten about the game.

'I'm calling it quits for this evening!' he shouted back. And to her, 'This is one helluva pointless trip you've made.'

'Do you think so?' The drive had taken longer than she had estimated. There had been traffic jams and detours, it had poured with rain all day, and when it grew dark and she had missed a couple of signposts along the by-roads, she had driven off in the wrong direction. In all the years that she had made plans to visit the village, something had always come up. Reinier's stubborn insistence that she went to Avezeel had begun to feel like an obligation. And after their divorce she had kept postponing it.

'I don't *think* it, I *know* it,' said the drug salesman, his amusement growing.

'What's the doctor like?' she asked.

'He's a decent fellow. A good old country doctor. Has his own pharmacy. Great client.'

'Has he lived here long?'

'Since before the war. Isn't that right, Sassing? You know that old pill-pedlar from way back, don't you?' He turned towards the innkeeper, but the man had just retreated into the kitchen.

'What's his name?'

'Dr Zegelrijke. Hey, why do you want to know? You're not by any chance in the pharmaceutical business, too? Planning to poach on my territory?' He was leaning half-way across the table by now.

'Of *course* not,' she said. She thought it was about time their conversation came to an end. When she saw that the innkeeper had reappeared behind the bar, she walked over to him. She ordered another whisky, picked up her travelling-bag and climbed the stairs.

2

The bulb hanging from a frayed wire in the corridor shone feebly, just enough for her to find the lock, which she succeeded in opening with some difficulty. As she shoved her bag into the room and switched on the light, she heard someone behind her.

'Throw that stuff in the sink! I've got much better whisky for you. Here you are, sweetheart, a whole bottle. Why don't we knock off this baby, just the two of us?'

It was the drug salesman. Holding up the bottle next to his splotchy red face, he forced himself into the doorway beside her and placed his other, empty hand on her shoulder. She smelled the thick reek of beer as he breathed against her cheek.

'Hey, are you mad? Get the hell out of here!' she jabbed her elbow into his stomach, slipped inside, slammed the door behind her and just managed to lock it before the man could push the handle down. Only when she had heard him walking away did she turn to face the room.

The long, narrow space was filled for the most part with two beds, piled high with quilts and cushions, that had been placed with their headboards against the wall. They barely allowed access to the window, where a gas heater was burning, which she immediately turned out, leaving only the pilot light flickering. She knelt down and examined the side of the convector, but she couldn't find a stopcock. Nauseated by the smell of gas, she got to her feet again and opened the window.

Her whisky appeared to have survived the incident at the door. She took a swig and began unpacking her bag. The same old travelling-bag – the leather was notched and peeling, the corners had been patched, the handles replaced, yet it still served her well. Reinier had often asked her why she didn't buy a new one. He thought it looked terrible. Fondly, she stroked the furrowed surface, as if she were fondling a pet. Should she let Reinier know that she was in Avezeel? If she called him, she might get Hilde on the phone, and that would require giving an up-to-the-minute account. She could always send him a postcard of the village with the name 'Maria' written on it. Would he still want to know? As far as he was concerned, that chapter of his life was closed. Hilde had been his psychotherapist; that was how they had met. She had helped him give up drinking. She was a spirited woman with whom he had probably felt more at ease in the past five years than he had in the twelve years of his marriage to Stella. He had been able to resume his teaching job, at a different school of course, but in his case that had been an advantage.

'Maria Roselier!' Reinier would suddenly exclaim.

He did it in season and out of season, sometimes while correcting papers, as if he were referring to one of his pupils. One evening he let slip the name in front of Charles, the young Dutch literature teacher who dropped in on them regularly, bringing her books of contemporary poetry and literary magazines in which various poems of his had been published.

'Maria Roselier! That's *her*, did you know that?' And he began telling him about her time in hiding; the places where she had lived, the false identity cards she had used; how, because of her, a dead girl from Zeeland had been restored to life. 'Do you think you can use this in your novel?' He drank down his sixth glass of gin and she saw that Charles, overwhelmed by a past about which she herself had never said a word, was growing more and more uneasy.

Had she been back since? No, nowhere. The polder? She wouldn't even be able to find the farm now. Charles suggested driving through the Haarlemmermeer; maybe she would recognize the spot. Reinier thought it an excellent idea. 'Take Maria Roselier out for a ride sometime, Charlie!'

'I wasn't called "Maria" when I lived in the polder, Reinier.'

'Oh, that's true. Her name then was Evelien.'

They had driven there in his red two-seater with the top down. It was the end of July and as hot as it had been in the summer of 1943. At first she felt completely relaxed, sitting there next to the tanned man in his white polo shirt. Now and then her long hair would flutter in his face, and he would nip at it. As they drove deeper into the farmland, along tree-lined roads verged with dense shrubbery, she realized that her fingers were curled tightly round the door handle. It had to be one of these roads. At a fork in the road, she was certain: they were very near. She recognized the farm. He stopped in front of the path, now paved, which led up to the yard. The roof looked as though it had been repaired, and seemed lower than she remembered it. The kitchen door no longer stood open. Would that stove still be burning? Neither in the yard nor in the field was there a soul in sight.

'Did you want to . . . '

'Just keep driving,' she said.

'Would you like to go to Haarlem?'

'Let's get out of the polder first.'

When they approached the city, he wanted to turn on to the road leading to the centre of town, but she placed her hand on his arm and shook her head. 'Don't bother.' He drove on to the dunes near Bloemendael, where in the warm breeze they lay among the reeds.

Their relationship had lasted for more than eight months. She enjoyed the suspense, the secret meetings, and at the same time was amazed at how easy it was, as if she had had years of experience behind her. After the first seven years with Reinier she sunk into a listlessness which she could not fight off and which he could do nothing to change. When she finally got over it, she thought she could no longer do without the excitement that her successive affairs had provided. She recovered her old energy. At school evenings – until then attended with the utmost reluctance, or avoided completely under all kinds of pretexts – she was always present. At one of these evenings she met a new colleague of Reinier's to whom she was attracted, just as she had been elsewhere to other men, in whom she thought she recognized features of former lovers. Time and again she seemed to be searching for an experience comparable to that single short-lived one of years before, as if she wanted to confirm her belief, once and for all, that it could not be equalled.

She brushed out her shoulder-length hair, trying to hide the grey streaks, but to no avail. She looked at the steadily deepening lines in her face, the heavy eyelids, the skin darkening under the sockets; and the images rose, the faces appeared. They had kept coming back to her, often at moments when she was least prepared: riding in her car through a deserted landscape or the crush of the city, in the middle of a conversation on a winter afternoon when the street-lamps were not yet lit and the light outside waned mercilessly; she saw them, now tangibly close, now totally unreachable. In her recurring dream, Carlo sometimes took the place of her father. Carlo, too, would be standing on the opposite side and moving towards the bridge – now delicate as a pencil drawing – while the distance between them remained unchanged.

Sitting on the edge of the bed, she drained her glass. The cotton curtain rippled, letting in the faint glow from a street-lamp. The room filled with the mingled odours of manure and humus, the same as she had smelled on the country road.

The rain had stopped when she had arrived in Avezeel. Before she knew what was happening she had left the village behind again and got stuck in cart-tracks that petered out at the foot of a fence. She had stepped out and peered across the dusky field at a couple of farms in the distance, their outlines already blurred into the dark trees around them. Then she had fixed her gaze on the village, like a film-maker who first scans his surroundings with his camera before zooming in on his target. Only a few contours had been visible to her, with that of the church steeple as a landmark.

Driving back slowly through the narrow streets she had found the village square, where, in the glare of the headlights, she had seen the card-players sitting behind the café window. Resolutely, she had walked inside, like an expected guest.

3

It had begun merely as a somewhat provocative mentioning of the name, but as the years passed Reinier spent more and more time conjecturing about Maria Roselier's background. What was he trying to insinuate? After all, he had no more information than she had. She usually ignored him on those occasions, instead of letting him see how much it annoyed her.

'It's about time you went to that village. You'll get to hear everything you want to know down there,' he said, yet again, as she sat at her desk working on the illustrations for a series of children's books. While he stood waiting in the doorway, she shifted her gaze to the high windows, to the crowns of the trees along the Amstel, the pale-blue sky above the Omval.

'I'm working now, Reinier. I have got to finish this. I've accepted the assignment and that's all there is to it.'

'And when you've finished this assignment, you'll find some other excuse. I know you will. You're always putting it off. You just let it keep bugging you – *and* me.' He came over to her; she could smell the liquor on his breath and see the burst blood-vessels in the whites of his eyes. 'I'm saying it for your own good, Stella, believe me, only for your own good.' He was looking past her as if he were addressing someone else.

They had reached a point in their marriage where they could no longer offer one another either comfort or support. He had begun drinking heavily and was having serious problems at school. She escaped into her affairs, a situation to which he had long resigned himself. She thought, now and then, about the early years of their relationship, the devotion, the almost bashful embraces of this man, ten years her senior, whom she had met through her downstairs neighbour.

'Are you still living here, Maria?!' Lina Retty had cried out in astonishment when she reappeared at the house a week after the Liberation. 'I got a lift from a couple of Canadians. I got this, too.' She placed a box on the table, full of tinned beef, meat and vegetables, powdered eggs, chocolates and cigarettes, and shared the goods generously. 'How did you make out during the *hongerwinter*?'[1]

'Oh, I managed.'

'Heard anything from your parents?'

'I've been making inquiries, but the lines are still down.' At that moment she had been unable to think of a different explanation. The other woman

[1] *hongerwinter*: literally, 'hunger winter', the Dutch term for the period of famine in the winter of 1944/5.

hadn't noticed a thing. But when Miss Retty heard from Mrs Benders just who had actually been living above her, she seemed shocked. Maria? In hiding? She must have realized what could have happened if it had been discovered during the Occupation, when she had known absolutely nothing about it. But she decided that something had to be arranged and swung into action, inquiring among her clients, going from one government agency to the next, until at last she showed up at Stella's door with the first lieutenant.

'This is Maria. She's been in hiding in *my* attic,' she had said proudly.

Ever since Stella had been to the Red Cross for news of her family and had left behind her address in case anyone was looking for her, she had kept her door open all day long so she could hear the front doorbell.

One morning there appeared to be a misunderstanding downstairs about someone who was supposedly living in the house. 'I'm afraid you're at the wrong place!' she heard Miss Retty call out. Leaning over the banister, she eavesdropped on their conversation.

'I was given this address,' said a woman's voice.

The front door slammed shut, footsteps sounded on the first flight of stairs. She knew whose they were.

'Where did you get it?' asked Miss Retty.

'From the Red Cross. Look, here. They wrote it down for me. This is the right address, isn't it?'

'Yes, only I don't know this person. There is a

student living here, but her name is Maria Roselier.'

'Why haven't you told her? Didn't you know everyone is revealing their real name now?' asked Mrs Benders as soon as she was upstairs. She sat down on the wicker chair and commented on the black-out paper that was still hanging over the window. That was no longer necessary, was it? Her face had grown white and puffy. For two years she had lived with her husband in a narrow, dark, windowless room. They hadn't once been outside.

'How did it happen? Where was it?'

'In Hilversum. They were apprehended in the street during a routine check and transported immediately.'

'Their identity cards weren't very good.'

'They were dreadful. I had warned Daniel so many times. He wouldn't listen to me, nor would Louise. It was totally safe, they said.'

'One didn't have much choice in those days.'

Mrs Benders had already been to the house where Daniel and Louise had lived for barely more than a year. Other people were living there. Everything had been stolen. They themselves had been able to move back into their house in Gouda, although that had also been plundered.

'Have you had any word about the others?'

'No, nothing.'

'It is complete and utter chaos in those offices,' sighed Mrs Benders. 'They are at their wits' end.' She fumbled through her purse. Stella averted her eyes; she looked at the table, at the writing-pad on which, in the last few months, she had not written a single letter.

'Is there any chance you might get something back?'

'I haven't looked into that yet.'

'Shall I send you some photographs?' With the handkerchief she had dug up out of her purse, Louise's mother dried her face, dabbed at her eyes and blew her nose.

'That will be fine.' She couldn't bring herself to say that she didn't want any photographs just yet.

'We must wait and see what happens.'

'Yes. It will take a long time before they know all the details, they told me at the Red Cross.'

'You never know.'

They were silent. Mrs Benders stood and walked to the door. On the landing, she asked, 'Is there anything I can do for you, Stella?'

Stella thanked her, said there was nothing she needed and that, for the time being, she wanted to stay in the attic room.

Kissing her hurriedly on the cheek, the little woman once again took out her handkerchief and blew her nose as she walked down the stairs. 'You are always welcome to visit us in Gouda,' she said before she left.

Stella placed a chair under the window, climbed on to it and yanked at the black-out paper so angrily that it ripped in half. The drawing-pins that had held it in place rained down on to the floor.

4

When Lina Retty had gone downstairs, he stepped farther into the room, so that his head, the hair cut short in the American fashion, practically touched the sloping wall. When he finally sat down – he had chosen one of the crates – he put his beret on the floor and took a packet of Sweet Caporal from the breast pocket of his battledress.

'Be my guest.'

'I don't smoke.'

'You're the first person I've heard say that since I've been in Amsterdam. Ever tried it?' Leaning forward, his elbows on his knees, he watched her warily.

'Once.'

He lit a cigarette, inhaled deeply, and seemed to have something on his mind. Did he feel he had landed in the middle of a situation he couldn't handle? Was he sorry he had allowed Miss Retty to talk him into coming?

'Looks to me like you're still in hiding.' He smiled as he said it.

'Then you've got the wrong impression. I've never

felt like that here.' She realized that the Liberation had scarcely altered her circumstances.

'But Miss Retty tells me you still call yourself "Maria Roselier".'

'I've got used to the name. I've had it since '43 and it's as if it's stuck to me. Do you find that strange?'

'Everybody's using their real names now, didn't you know that? There's no reason to hide them any more.'

'I know that.' He was just repeating what Mrs Benders had said.

'Are you scared?'

'I was seldom scared during the war, and I'm not scared now either.' She made a fist and pounded it into the palm of her left hand. There was another fear, a fear she could not talk about.

'Then who are you hiding from? From yourself? What is your name?'

'Would you like to know how I found out that we'd been liberated?' She turned her chair so that she was sitting diagonally opposite him. 'I'd pulled up the black-out curtain and I saw a man leaning out of an attic window, just like mine, across the street. He had long white hair and a yellowish face. He started flapping his arms up and down, as hard as he could, like someone shaking a blanket. It was as if he'd been waiting for me to show my face at the window. At first I didn't know what he meant. I thought he was a bit soft in the head. But then I heard all the racket downstairs and I saw more and more people coming out into the street. They were pushing, pulling, slapping each other on the shoulders, dancing and laughing – it was like a carnival. When they saw me, they waved and shouted that we'd been freed.' Her throat had become so dry that she walked to the sink and held her mouth under the tap. The water trickled down her neck.

'What did you do? Did you go outside?'

'Going outside was nothing new for me.'

'But it was different then, wasn't it?'

'Yes, of course. Everyone had gone berserk.'

'And did you walk into town?'

'Of course, all the way to the Dam. I saw everything.' It was clear to her that he was not asking questions out of mere curiosity.

She had phoned Roelofs; she couldn't think of anyone else. Even more so than the time before, she had had to overcome her aversion as she dialled the number. The first week she was unable to get through, but she had no desire to go to his house. As soon as she heard that the telephones were working again, she made another attempt.

'You're the first person to ring!' he had yelled into the telephone. 'That's promising. Come along over here! We've just started on the orange bitters. I've been drunk for two weeks running.'

'What do you know about Carlo?' she had asked. He was silent for a moment, then said that Carlo had been arrested. From the prison in Scheveningen he had been transported to Vught and later sent on to a camp in Germany. 'Dachau, I think.' He offered to look into it for her, but she said she could do so herself.

'Why don't you come over first?'

She had hung up.

'Do you have anywhere to go to?' asked the officer.

'I'll be staying here for now. This has been my home for years.'

He nodded understandingly and stood up. 'It wouldn't do you any harm to go out once in a while. Call me if you feel like it.' He wrote something on a card and handed it to her.

'How did you actually end up in the British army? Were you involved in the Underground?'

'I went west with the Allied troops. I was a reserve lieutenant and joined up with the British during the Battle of Arnhem. Later, I became one of their liaison officers.'

'Had you been in hiding, too?'

'Yes, you could say so, though I saw it more as a change of address. When we were made prisoners of war for the second time, I got away. I hope I can get a job again soon at my old school.'

'At a school?'

'I'm a history teacher.'

Shortly after he left she looked at his card. *Reinier Varendonk* it said, with a telephone number written underneath. This time she wouln't have to memorize it.

5

The table where she had sat the evening before had been laid for breakfast, which was brought by a girl of about sixteen with short black hair and dark-brown eyes. At the other window sat a Flemish-speaking couple. The man, licking his lips, dipped a crust of bread into the yolk of his fried egg. To her relief, the drug salesman was not there. While the girl was pouring coffee for her, she asked for directions to the doctor's house.

'It's easy to get there. But you'd better wait and ask my father. He's busy at the moment.' She pointed outside, where Sassing was washing his car.

When Stella left the hotel, the man had exchanged his sponge and chamois for a bit of cotton waste. Barely glancing at her, he indicated the way: it was on the outskirts of the village. For a moment she considered asking him again about Maria, but the exaggerated attention he was giving to the chromium-plate of his bumper discouraged her from doing so. The weather had cleared up; the sun was shining through the chestnut trees on to the rounded cobblestones in the square, which still glistened with rainwater. Brown leaves lay in the gutters, blown together during the rainstorm.

Dr Zegelrijke's waiting-room was located in an extension at the back of his imposing house. It had one wall made entirely of glass, which provided a view of meadows enclosed by a grassy bank topped with a row of elm trees. She had telephoned to say that she was eager to speak to him, but that it wasn't about an appointment. She was told that she could come immediately.

The doctor, a wiry man with a high forehead and a halo of woolly grey hair, watched her expectantly from behind his desk. Her father would have been about the same age now. She had difficulty imagining this. Through the years her memories of him had gradually concentrated themselves into one image: the unmoving, lost, unapproachable figure on the ice-covered bridge.

'I wanted to ask you whether you could tell me anything about Maria Roselier.'

'Maria Roselier,' he repeated slowly. His hands, spread out on the blotter, began rearranging the already meticulously arranged objects within their reach: a stethoscope, a crystal paperweight, a silver picture-frame. 'Are you perhaps a relative of hers?'

'No, no.'

'Did you know her, then?'

'No, that's not it either. You might find this strange, but I've always been curious about her. The fact that I know nothing about her has obsessed me for a long time.' The back of the picture-frame was made of black cardboard, with an easel of the same material. It reminded her of the picture-frames her parents would place on the sideboard whenever her grandparents were coming to visit them. They appreciated having the entire family 'on display' during their stay. Often the cardboard easels would be crooked or in need of regluing. 'For years I'd been planning to come to Avezeel. My plans never materialized. Finally, yesterday, I forced myself to get into my car and drive down. At the hotel I heard you'd been in practice here for a long time, and that's when I thought of coming to ask you some questions. A doctor in a small village like this one is bound to be up to date on everything.'

'He is up to date on many things, but there is very little he can permit himself to talk about. Probably they have not been too helpful at the hotel either, have they?'

'No, not at all. I get the impression that people around here are rather reluctant to talk.'

'Yes. Especially concerning delicate matters.' He moved a pad to the edge of the blotter. 'But, wait a minute – would you happen to be the person who was given Maria Roselier's identity card during the war?'

'You know about that?'

'Oh yes. We had a civil servant working in the Registry who switched identity cards for the Underground. You've probably heard about this sort of thing since then. It happened in other towns as well. The boys did the rest. They managed to provide many, many people in hiding with proper documents. I thought they were taking enough risks, without – ah, well. . . .' They both looked outside. Drifting clouds cast long shadows across the meadow. A magpie hopped from the roof of a shed to a white garden seat.

'Does the name "Carlo" mean anything to you?' she asked.

'Certainly. "Carlo" was the code name of a young man in the Resistance.'

She had not expected this. Now at last she understood his urging: 'When the war is over, go down to Avezeel sometime.' 'His name was Laurens,' she heard the doctor saying. She knew it. And she also knew, hearing his real name for the first time, that to her he would always be Carlo.

Dr Zegelrijke picked up the picture-frame and turned it round. 'This is my son Guus,' he said. She saw a young man with a round, smiling face. He had slightly protruding teeth and his light-blond hair was parted in the middle. 'Guus and Laurens were classmates. They joined the Students' Resistance Movement early on, in Amsterdam. In the middle of January 1943 Guus walked into an SD[1] trap in Amsterdam Central Station. A month later they arrested Laurens, in Rotterdam, with a bag full of ration cards and blank identity cards. He'd been to see me just a few days before. Guus's arrest had been a great shock to him. He suspected treachery had been involved, but despite my warnings he was determined to carry on. "The work must be done." I can still hear him saying that.' He put the portrait

---

[1] SD = Sicherheitsdienst: German security services.

back in its place. 'Like so many others, they did not survive.'

Besides Mrs Benders, Jaap, the eldest of the three Boston brothers, was the only person she had seen again. Apparently he had not been in the house that Saturday afternoon. On his way home a neighbourhood acquaintance had told him that they had cordoned off the street and were clearing the houses. With the help of his friend the antiquarian bookseller, he had been able to go into hiding. She had run into him several months after the Liberation, in the Stadsschouwburg, where Charlotte Köhler was giving her first reading since before the war. As she and Reinier,who had begun taking her out regularly, were walking to their seats, she had felt a hand on her shoulder. Someone had asked, 'Stella? Is that you?' She had started. Even before she had turned round she had recognized the voice. 'Mr Boston!' She had never called him by his first name, and only rarely had a conversation with him. In the past, whenever she had returned one of his books, he had promptly given her a new one, saying, 'Now you must read this.' He had kept her at a distance. It was as if he had been interested solely in determining the sequence of her reading matter. But this time he embraced her, and Reinier switched places with him so that they could sit next to each other. Every so often he caught her hand and clasped it tightly; she had difficulty in concentrating on the reading, catching only fragments of the Song of Solomon, '. . . I sought him, but I could not find him . . . . I called him, but he gave me no answer . . . .

The watchmen that went about the city found me, they smote me, they wounded me. . . .'

The doctor had pushed his chair away from the table and walked to the window. 'If you stand here, you can see the house where the Roseliers used to live.' In the clear morning light she saw a red-brown roof behind the elms. 'Shall we drive over there?' asked Dr Zegelrijke.

_____

6

'It was as if somebody had hurled a brick into a
pond. And as you've noticed, after all these years
the ripples are still there, as if they'd been frozen
in motion,' he said. He had invited Stella to drop
in again some time after office hours, but Stella
had not come back. She had heard enough, seen
enough. Driving along the narrow roads of Zeeusch-
Vlaanderen towards Breskens, she remembered the
disappointment she had felt when she had finally
stood in front of the house where Maria Roselier
had lived. What she saw had in no way resembled
what she had imagined. It was a middle-class home,
clearly renovated, with a garden round it that was
kept in check by rows of white stones and plenty of
white gravel. The shed had caught her eye, though,
its large windows covering the entire width of the
roof.

When the Roseliers had moved away after the
incident, the house had remained empty for a long
time; no one wanted to live in it, and it fell rapidly
into disrepair. 'Then, about ten years ago, they were
spotted again, here in the neighbourhood. It was

the middle of winter, it had snowed lightly and towards evening it began to freeze over. They hadn't been visiting anyone, and no one had seen them in the village during the day. Later we heard that they had settled in France after the war. Whatever reason they had for returning to Avezeel, has never been explained. All we know is that they were heading for Terneuzen. When they got to the Avezeelse Vlakte their car skidded, slid down a bank and landed in the canal. They'd practically been forgotten around here. That accident stirred things up all over again.'

A few hundred yards past the house he turned into a side-road that ran through a marshy field. Now that she was here, he thought they might as well drive down to the creek. Stella had no idea what she would see there. It brought on a feeling of tension which, until then, had somehow been missing. The doctor's rather disjointed account was partly responsible. He seemed to be having trouble relating it.

'The Roseliers were real outsiders. The man was a painter and his wife made wall hangings. The life they led ran contrary to everything that the people in the village were accustomed to. Artists, and foreign ones at that – the villagers were not terribly fond of them. I had the impression that the Roseliers were not without means. They could afford small luxuries, they took frequent trips, and then Maria would be left behind, by herself.' He told her that Maria had often been sick as a child. 'She was vulnerable to tuberculosis.' When Stella suggested that this must have been the cause of Maria's untimely death, he shook his head. 'No, no, I'd treated her right from childhood. She had grown out of it quite nicely. She had become – how shall I put it – tougher.' It seemed that Maria had also had artistic talent. She drew, and painted water-colours, mostly of birds. With her sketch-book and her binoculars she sat, almost every day, on the little island in the creek, where there was a little hut among the reeds which had formerly been used by poachers and fishermen.

'She spent a lot of time with Sassing's son. You've seen him. He took over the hotel from his father. The boy also was a bird-watcher. One often saw them rowing together up the creek. They were apparently planning to marry, but his parents were opposed to it. When mobilization was announced, Sassing had to join the army. He was stationed in Bergen op Zoom, and whenever he was on leave, rain or shine, he and Maria would go to the island. They took refuge in the hut. At the beginning of April 1940 a Greek freighter collided with a groyne in the canal. The *Evgenia* – I don't know why I still remember the name – was badly damaged. Repairs would take several weeks. You couldn't keep Maria away from the site. She had fallen in love with one of the crew, the third helmsman. One day Sassing came home on leave unexpectedly, and caught the two of them in the hut.'

They had parked by the side of the creek, a pool of water with a jagged shoreline fringed with reeds. Dr Zegelrijke pointed to a small building across the water, reachable by way of a narrow pier, where canoes and flat boats were moored. 'You're out of luck. The café is only open in the summer.' The windows were shuttered and above the entrance she saw a sign with the words *The Curlew*. 'It ended in a brawl. Sassing dragged the helmsman across the footbridge that was still there at the time, and practically threw him on to the road. Maria jumped into the water and swam ashore.'

Stella had rolled down the car window. The autumn sun was mirrored in the pool, which teemed with brown ducks. 'Couldn't she have escaped across the bridge?'

'Sassing must have barred the way – and knowing Maria, she wouldn't have hesitated for a moment. She was extremely impulsive. She often acted without thinking. That's why she had flung herself into the affair in the first place.'

'April . . . the icy water . . . was that the reason?'

'Maria's swim to safety was not without its consequences. She caught pneumonia. As I told you earlier, she was tough. And if we'd had the medicines then that are available now, she would definitely have recovered. She succumbed to pleurisy on the second day of the war, just as the French troops were crossing our border.' He started the car. It was time for him to return to his patients. 'The following year Sassing tore the hut down,' he said on the way home. 'It was no great loss. Later they built the café in its place.'

They had parted at the entrance to the doctor's house. When he was half-way down the garden path, he had turned suddenly and walked over to her again. 'When Guus and Laurens told me that they were going to use Maria's name for an identity card, I said to them, "You can't do that. Leave her in peace. Think of someone else." But they did it anyway. "It's just the card we need," Laurens said. There was no alternative, not here. I knew that only too well. And you – it helped you. For you it was a godsend.'

'Yes,' she had said, 'it certainly was.'

Only when she was standing on the ferry did Stella realize that she had not even asked the doctor what Maria had looked like. But after all she had heard, she decided to hold on to the impression she had formed of her years before, the one she had come to know so well.

She walked to the edge of the deck, her hair blown back and her face growing damp in the quickly gathering mist. With both hands on the railing, the travelling-bag against her legs, she remained standing there until, in the glimmer of late afternoon, she saw the lights of Vlissingen appearing on the horizon.